*...ost the second my eyes rested on him, he turned his head
...d looked at me. For a moment I couldn't breathe, as if I'd
...mped into cold water. I could say it was like a searchlight,
...icking me out in the crowd, except that there was nothing light
about it. Imagine a beam not of light but of dark, so concentrated
that it dazzles you: you have to look away. And when I blinked
and looked back he was gone.*

Nick is desperate—out on the streets, in a strange town,
with no money, no ID. That's when he sees Swan and the
other human statues—street performers who can turn
themselves, almost, to stone. Maybe he can do that? He's
got nothing to lose—has he?

Somewhere in the shadows, watching him, is Antonin,
with his offer of a place at his secret academy of
'immobilists'. Inside its high walls and locked gates, Nick
and Swan are drawn into a claustrophobic world, more like
a cult than a theatre school. Over it all presides Antonin,
who has gone further than anybody should in his 'going
for stone'. Is it already too late when Nick starts to sense
the kind of danger he and Swan are in?

Philip Gross was born in Cornwall in 1952, the son of an
Estonian wartime refugee and a Cornish schoolmaster's
daughter. He has won several prizes for his poetry and his
collection *The Wasting Game* was shortlisted for the Whitbread
Poetry Prize in 1998. He now teaches Creative Writing at Bath
Spa University College and lives in Bristol. *Going for Stone* is his
first novel for Oxford University Press.

Going For Stone

Going For Stone

Philip Gross

OXFORD
UNIVERSITY PRESS

OXFORD
UNIVERSITY PRESS

Great Clarendon Street, Oxford OX2 6DP

Oxford University Press is a department of the University of Oxford.
It furthers the University's objective of excellence in research, scholarship,
and education by publishing worldwide in

Oxford New York

Auckland Bangkok Buenos Aires
Cape Town Chennai Dar es Salaam Delhi Hong Kong Istanbul
Karachi Kolkata Kuala Lumpur Madrid Melbourne Mexico City Mumbai
Nairobi São Paulo Shanghai Taipei Tokyo Toronto

Oxford is a registered trade mark of Oxford University Press
in the UK and in certain other countries

British Library Cataloguing in Publication Data available

ISBN 0 19 271905 X

1 3 5 7 9 10 8 6 4 2

Typeset by AFS Image Setters Ltd, Glasgow

Printed in Great Britain by Mackays of Chatham plc, Chatham, Kent

'Mum, Mum! Is it real?'

There's a little kid watching, can't be more than five or six—too young to be clever about this kind of thing, but they do have instincts. His instincts say: 'There's something wrong here. Something very wrong.' He's staring, eyes wide, and gripping his mother's hand. She's got things to attend to, places to go; she's trying to pull him away but it's as if he's turned to concrete, bolted to the spot—she can't budge him. He's stiff as a statue himself.

'Mmmmaaaam . . . ' His mouth comes open in a low wail. 'Maaaaam. I saw it blink.'

The mother stops tugging. She's quite young, as mums go, with soft curly hair and a tired pretty face; she's all powdery colours. I take all this in as she turns, and stops, and looks, and her eyes meet mine. She's been going to snap, 'Of course it's not real! Don't be silly.' But she hesitates, and for a moment I can see she doesn't know. That's what gets me, that split second as her eyes, her big blue eyes, go wider and she knows why the kid is whingeing. That's the kick. I don't like to admit it, but it makes my heart beat faster, even now.

Look, she's staring at me like our parents told us never never to do. She can't make sense of it . . . If she decides it is a statue, she'll think: very clever, almost too good to be true. But what if it isn't . . . ? Then she'll be staring, can't look away, at a living person, one who's staring back at her, cold and unblinking as stone.

It could be worse—though she won't think this; she's not been to the places I've been or seen what I've seen. Worse still is it's not quite one thing or the other, not quite real or pretend, not flesh not stone but something in between.

1

The moment lasts too long. My eyes are stinging with the effort. Then I blink. She flinches and turns away sharply, whisking the kid away with her, as if the whole thing's been a nasty joke. A few steps on, they stop. She ferrets in her handbag, quick and clumsy, then pushes some coins in his hand. The kid dodges back, looking down, not at me. He throws the pennies in the hat, turns so fast he almost trips, and runs after her.

That's how it works. She's got to give something, like protection money. If she doesn't, she'll be thinking about that moment the rest of the day. She'll be wondering when the kid will wake up, that night or the next night or not for months or years, with a nightmare about statues that have human eyes that blink. Now she's paid me—about thirteen pence, as far as I could hear without looking—and she thinks that sets her free.

1

It all came crashing down around me. They'll talk about a 'broken home' but what's the big deal these days? Half the families I know are built from the pieces of other ones, and they rub along together. They sort it out somehow—who's whose step-brother, whose half-sister and whose ex. But when I say 'crashing down' I mean it.

Malcolm needn't have been a bad thing. It had been a few years since Dad, but we weren't sitting round moping about it; Mum was getting on with things. I had to agree with her: it was kind of a relief when Dad finally left, the way he'd mooned about the place towards the end. Still, she needed someone there to chivvy about a bit, and there was only me, and I was going out more, like you do when you're nearly sixteen. Most nights there'd be something, a rehearsal at Young Stagers or just a few of us meeting round a friend's house, watching a video, hanging out. Then I'd poke my head in round the door to Mum: 'OK if I go to so-and-so's?' She'd say yes with that look that meant that actually she'd got something special for our supper. Ah well, she'd say, never mind. Sometimes I'd stay in when she said that—she's my mum, after all—and then she'd get guilty about it. It was a bit of a strain all round. So when Malcolm turned up that was fine by me. She started sprucing herself up. I'd catch her smiling in the mirror. She started shopping again and got some nice things, for her age. Malcolm must have liked that. He was into ties—a jacket, shirt, and tie and, wait for it, cufflinks and tiepin in a matching set.

Don't believe what I say about Malcolm, by the way. He was just the opposite to Dad, that's all, the absolute black-and-white, upside-down, inside-out polar opposite. I suppose that's what Mum went for. I'm just telling you the way it looked to me, sixteen. I was restless, dead restless, and not in a mood to be pleased.

The first time I met Malcolm he gave me a lecture, starting with a question: what did I have in mind as a career? I shrugged, the way you do, and watched him. I knew why he was asking. I'd just told Mum what my plans were, now that the exams were over. I knew I'd done OK. But no way was I going through another couple of years of school. I was ready for a change.

'Now, take me. I could have been stuck in a dead end job . . . ' said Malcolm. He'd got it wrong, of course. They did the Art and the Spanish I wanted at the college, and I could do Theatre Studies too. And I could have said that, only . . . it was the fact that she'd told him. They'd been sorting my life out for me, behind my back. And now this. 'Take me,' he said. 'I got my act together. I smartened up.'

It was Friday nights at first. Malcolm came round for a meal. So we could get to know each other, Mum said. After the coffee and thin mints—no joke: we never even used to have *afters*—there'd be the meaningful question, then 'Take me, now . . . ' Take me, I used to be Mr Nice Guy, till I realized the others were all out for what they could get. Take me, I wasn't in line for that promotion, but I saw my chance. It's dog eat dog out there, you mark my words. Take me . . .

No thanks. I don't believe he'd ever been Mr Nice Guy. Even at school he'd have been the kind of kid that sells you cigarettes behind the bike shed, and when the

4

teacher catches you he's nowhere to be seen. No, I didn't take to Malcolm, but . . . oh, I guess I can see why Mum did. He had energy. He was going somewhere. He didn't just talk, he made things happen, the way Mum liked to. I guess she should have married a bloke like him in the first place. Then again, if she had, what would I have been like? I mean: would I have . . . no, I mean: who would he have been, their kid, who'd have lived in my bedroom and called himself me?

That's enough of that. And enough of the Understanding Malcolm business, too. It was when he moved his car in that it came to blows.

He had a little white Lotus, a low open-top thing with too much leather, with headlights like a frog's eyes, and it gleamed, it always gleamed as if he'd polished it that day. Needless to say, he couldn't leave it in the street, not in a neighbourhood like ours, so he got Mum to tell me I'd have to clear the garage. It just happened that there was a new production on that week at the Stagers, and we'd painted some flats for the scenery—really big ones, and they needed somewhere safe to dry. Well, I tidied back a skip-load of rubbish, old paint cans and the rest of it, but I pushed the flats against the wall. Which is where they would have stayed, if Malcolm hadn't swept his little white number in with lots of revving, to impress Mum. It must have been the door that caught one of the flats; at any rate it toppled over quietly behind him and when he went out in the morning, there was a bit of the backdrop from *The Tempest* printed in oil paint inside out along one door.

Well, of course he went volcanic, hauled me out of bed and downstairs to find the sets dragged out and one of the panels kicked in, not quite by accident. In the shouting match that followed I happened to say something like 'It's only a car'. That's when he hit me. Not hard, but he meant

5

it. I could see him quivering. In the long long pause that followed, no one moved and I waited for Mum to say something . . . and I waited, and she didn't. She just kind of froze, as if something had jammed inside her. I wanted to shake her but I couldn't move either. All I could do was look at her, and she knew I was looking but she wouldn't meet my eyes.

I was up in my bedroom when she came up later. 'Nick,' she said, 'Nick, there's something I should tell you.'

That you're sorry? I thought. That those rose-tinted glasses of hers went smash at the second Malcolm hit me? I turned to face her, hopeful . . . and I knew with a sick sort of feeling in my stomach that it wasn't going to be like that.

'Nick . . . ' she said again. She sat down on a tiny corner of my bed. Now I looked, I could see she was pale, and slightly shaking. 'I know it isn't easy but, Nick, it's really important that we . . . all try to get on together. Because Malcolm and me . . . I was going to tell you this at . . . at a better moment, but . . . we're going to have a baby. Nick? Please try to understand . . . '

So that was that. Imagine it, go on: how would *you* feel? For me, at that moment, it was as if I was watching myself from a distance, on a film that was quiet and slow, and there's a voice-over saying: 'It was then that Nick knew he was going to leave home.' Before Mum had even stumbled to the end of the sentence I was glancing round the bedroom, packing a suitcase in my mind. In the very first moment I'd seen myself storming out, slam, there and then. But no, I'd have looked like a kid in a tantrum. Then the voice-over feeling came down round me, sort of cold and clear. I would go. But not just yet. It would take some planning, and a cool head.

I got hold of an address—Dawn and Gareth, two of the drama lot who'd moved away the year before. They'd liked me and they always said, 'If ever you're up our way, just call.' So I would. Not a word to anybody, though, not anyone at all. That was the hard part. I'm not one of those people who's got to be trading inmost secrets with a best friend or a bunch of mates. Self-contained, that's what they say about me mostly. But it was hard, sitting up in my bedroom, gazing at some of the posters, getting really tatty round the edges, that I'd woken up to every morning since I was a kid. I mean: that one from the dinosaur museum, side by side with the girl in the wet-jeans advert, a Young Stagers production or two, and the clubs and the bands. I tried to imagine tacking up my little treasures in the corner of an attic, if they had one, in Gareth and Dawn's house. Pathetic. You can't take it with you, they say—though they're usually talking about dying. All of this stuff belonged here, in this life, where I wouldn't be.

It was too much to think all at once. I lay back and stared at the ceiling. I clicked the light off. As I did, it was black for a moment, then there was a scattering of bits of glow-worm green. I gazed at the glow-stars, little luminous sticky-back things from the toy shop, that Dad had brought home when I was ten. I couldn't help smiling at the thought of him, up a step-ladder, with a star map in the other hand, trying to make the constellations. He was between jobs at the time—that's how we had to put it—and I guess he was pretty low, and Mum was losing patience. While he was up that ladder, though, with the glow-stars, he kind of forgot himself and glowed a little, too. Then he got carried away with Orion, and gave him long stick legs and big feet, and we both started laughing. He laughed till the steps began to wobble and I held them steady for him. I can feel the wobble in my hands right now.

That next week, though . . . It passed like an ice age. Sometimes I wanted to write a letter to myself and post it, just so I could tell *somebody*. I got scared I might start talking in my sleep. But I mustn't let a word slip to anyone. Mum knew most of my friends round here and she would be on to them as soon as she realized I'd gone. Malcolm wouldn't be far behind her, either, after what I'd got planned for his car.

2

The elegant thing was that I didn't even touch it, much as I'd have loved to trash the thing in person. It would be when he'd swanned out after breakfast, in a hurry for some most important meeting, when he'd rattled up the up-and-over garage door, that he dislodged the brick that would do for the windscreen and the bonnet, and the pots of paint to put the white bits and the leather upholstery pretty well beyond repair. I put in some bags of nails and bits of metal just for effect, and it would almost have been worth sticking round to hear the crash. Almost. I'm not stupid. I was on the early-morning coach when it happened, but I'd been careful to book a different trip as well, to London, and to leave the receipt for it lying in a place they'd find it in an hour or two. That left a hole in my none-too-healthy bank account, but it would get them on the wrong track. I emptied what was left out of the account in case they tried to trace me that way. I'm not stupid, like I said.

I imagined that crash, though. There I was staring out of the coach window on some bypass somewhere and inside my head the whole thing unreeled like a film. If there'd been an audience they'd have cried with laughter. I must have chuckled a little, because the woman in the next seat started giving me looks. I gave her a vague grin back. No, I had to be careful. Not friendly, not unfriendly—the best thing I could be now was invisible.

There, that's the family history out of the way. Don't worry, I'm not going to waste my time whingeing: look

9

what happened to poor me because of my family, etcetera. I don't even wish it hadn't happened . . . which seems crazy, considering what did. Maybe I mean I can't imagine any more the kid I used to be, or who I would have been if not for all of it. What matters is that one day there I was, in the bus station in a strange town, getting off the coach, and rooting around in my pockets, figuring how long the cash I had would last. Not long. I got myself a coffee at the snack canteen, and spooned five or six sugars in, as sweet as I could stand. I needed every gram of energy I could get. To find Dawn and Gareth's, that was all I had to do. All those hours on the coach had left me ragged, though I'd slept a bit. Maybe I'd have been better off not sleeping, because every bump jerked me awake. Now I was crumpled, with a crick in my neck. I must have looked desperate, because of what happened next.

I'd been looking in the bookshop window, doing sums. Could I afford a street map? No, I'd just have to ask. There was this couple coming my way—well-off twenty-somethings who might have been a pair of young estate agents, that sort of smart. I just opened my mouth to say, 'Excuse me, can you tell me the way . . . ?' His face slammed shut. A moment earlier he'd been all smiles, telling her some killing little joke.

'Get a job,' he muttered, pulling his little lady closer. 'Beggars everywhere,' he said, louder, as they went by. 'Sweep them off the streets, that's what I'd do. They only want it for the drugs. It's a disgrace.'

So that was it. I hadn't got as far as the *'Excuse me . . .'* For a moment I just stood there with a sort of cold flush through my body and my mouth still hanging open, and I couldn't move at all.

I blinked and the couple had gone. The crowd flowed by

around me—strangers, all of them, shoppers with their heads down, pushing on, or tourists looking round them in a kind of glassy daze. None of them gave a toss about me. Back home, they might have the police out by now. Would they? Maybe Malcolm would rather be the one who caught me, so he could sort me out in his own way. That was a bad thought. Then again, maybe he'd be happier just to see me gone.

But the estate agent couple, they'd seen me. What if they'd been friends of Malcolm's or my mum? No, they hadn't seen *me*. They'd seen what they were expecting, just a beggar—and I hadn't even dressed to look the part. It hit me with a little shudder: I *was* invisible. And that meant I could be whatever else I chose to be.

My heart was beating faster. I went with the crowd, not thinking yet where I was going. I was a bit high with it, threading among them, noticing the faces while they didn't notice me—just a second on each, enough to clock them, which ones looked determined, which ones vacant, which ones sad. I understood how a pickpocket does it—like a member of another species, passing among the ones he preys on, in disguise.

That's when I saw the Saints. I don't know what it was that made me stop and look. Maybe there was a slight hitch in the movement of the crowd around them; people glanced and hesitated, then moved on. They were stone-coloured, the Saints, even down to the blotches of greyish lichen, like the walls behind them; they were still, but they weren't in their niches—one each, in the wall of the church behind them—but on the pavement, and one of them was leaning forward, very carefully dabbing at some detail of the make-up round the other's eye. The second one opened his eyes wide and blinked, so I saw the pink rims and their whites. The first one nodded, and they both smiled. In the second it took me to clock this, they turned and stepped into their niches, and were stone.

I found Dawn and Gareth's. It was not, as my mum would have said, a nice area. It was quite a long walk from the centre, out of the office blocks and shops, and there was a Kwik-Fit tyre warehouse at the end of the road. All the houses looked tatty, but the one I was after, number 25, looked derelict. One of the upstairs window panes had gone and was blocked with a piece of hardboard. There were curtains of a kind, but you could see they were bits of sheet and old bedspread, tacked up somehow. The wheelie bin had emptied itself on the patch of front garden. There was a faded leaflet in the window, with a black and white picture of a cat with its head in a steel clamp and Protest Against Live Experiments and a date some time last year. There was no bell or knocker. I banged on the door.

Somewhere inside there was music. After a minute or two, I banged again, and kept banging until the upstairs window opened. The head that looked out had a bit of a beard and mousy dreadlocks. 'Yeah?' it said. He listened blankly, so I wasn't quite sure if he'd heard me, then turned and shouted back into the house. 'Some kid says he's a friend of Dawn and Gareth. Anyone called Dawn and Gareth here?' There was a long pause, and for the first time I felt a little lurch inside me. What if the answer was just No?

'No,' the head said and vanished. The window slammed.

I stared at the upended wheelie bin, and the spill of cans and takeaway cartons and wads of free newspapers, well sodden down with the rain, and the usual adverts, envelopes and things. Near the top was a letter from the electricity company; I could see the red print through the window. A Final Demand. The name on it was Dawn's.

12

I hammered on the door again, and went on hammering.

Someone relented in there, because five minutes later I was in what might have been a living room. The man with dreads was there, and a woman with studs and pink hair, though she wasn't young, and a couple of others. There were two or three mattresses across the floor; someone had been at the wall with a can of spray paint, then down to the carpet and the mattresses as well. Yes, someone remembered that someone had said there'd been a Dawn and Gareth—the last tenants, like—but they'd gone.

'Gone?' I said. 'Where?'

The others shrugged. There must have been something in the way I looked then, because the woman with the pink hair said, 'You on the run, then?' She waved vaguely in the direction of one of the mattresses. 'Suppose you'd better stay.' And that was that. Nobody mentioned what their names were. Then again, none of them ever asked me mine.

It was late that night it struck me that I was in shock. I felt numb and tired all over and I started yawning, yawning. All day I'd been buzzing, feeling edgy and hyper-alert; now suddenly I crashed. I sat on a mattress in the upstairs room at the back, the only room that no one else was sleeping in, and picked at the bag of chips I'd let go cold in my hand. I stared out of the window, and felt low.

Dawn and Gareth had gone. They'd left no address; someone thought they remembered someone else saying that the previous tenants had owed the landlord a bundle of rent and done a moonlight flit. Nobody here now knew them, and most of them didn't know each other, either. The place was a squat. About a dozen of them drifted in and out, and some time towards midnight someone came back with word that there was a free party starting up

13

across town, and most of them vanished. I don't know if I was invited, but I didn't care.

It did cross my mind that I could just go home. I tried to imagine myself back there, knocking on the door, praying it would be Mum who answered. If it was, I'd have about a minute to make her understand, before Malcolm came downstairs and saw me. I tried to imagine . . . but all I could see was her face that day he'd hit me, and the way she wouldn't meet my eyes.

If I'd been feeling low like this at home, I'd have dropped round to some friend or other's. They're a good crowd, and we used to laugh a lot—like when I'd launch into one of those *What-if?* thoughts that hit you sometimes: What if we're only dreaming there's a real world around us? What if you're only imagining me, or *I*'m imagining *you*? The others would laugh and say: 'Deep, Nick, really deep.' But that was a hundred miles away and besides . . . With a shock I realized that of all of them—I said their names over in my mind, and it sounded like a foreign language—there was none of them I'd trust with this.

Outside, there was the town, or the glow of it behind the wires and roof tops. What had I hoped would happen if Dawn and Gareth *had* been here? I couldn't think now. Then a picture floated back into my mind, like the start of a dream. The Stone Saints, one taking care of the other one's make-up with the kind of touch a mother has, leaning over her toddler wiping something off his face: keep still . . . there! I didn't even know if they were men or women underneath their coat of stone-paint, but I couldn't forget that moment. One minute they were stone, the next so human.

They had money, though. There were coins in their collecting hat. Was it a job, or pocket money? I was going to need money, and I'd need it soon. Enough of the finer feelings—it was time I got thinking. There was bound to be a job in a fast-food joint somewhere, or a service station, somewhere they wouldn't ask too many questions about my age. Everybody says that I can pass for eighteen, easy. So that's what I'd do in the morning. I lay back on the lumpy dampness of the mattress, telling myself I had a plan, telling myself again and again until, without noticing, I fell asleep.

I've always had blockbuster dreams. I used to annoy my mates when they were going on about the latest Playstation game: I'd tell them that my dreams were better. In this one, I was running but the crowd was in my way; they'd stopped to gawp at the Stone Saints. Malcolm was after me, him and the police, and some of the teachers from school, and Mum and the social services too. There was a police car going nee-naw, trying to push through. If I could go still, as still as the Saints, then I'd become invisible, the way rabbits freeze when a hawk passes over. They know the hawk's eyes only lock on to movement; one twitch of your whiskers and you're dead. I froze. But there in the thick of the crowd was a shape I thought I . . . Yes: that head and shoulders, with a slight stoop and a certain way of moving. 'Dad!' I called. He turned. It wasn't him. And everybody else turned too. A space cleared round me, and a ring of staring faces. One of them was Malcolm's.

There was a creak behind me, as the Stone Saints came alive. They blinked, and bowed a slow bow. In the same slow movement they turned to each other, laid hold of the pillars on the wall between them, and began to pull. There was a creaking, then a shudder, as something deep inside the building gave way. A crack began to open, just a finger's width at first, and it seemed as if it would snap back in place, but the two stone figures braced themselves and pulled, and pulled, and I ran for the opening. There was a grinding sound, and stone-dust raining down around us. Just as I leaped for it the crack went zigzag up the frontage. The crowd were suddenly screaming, fighting their way over each other in panic, as blocks of stone and gargoyles hit the pavement and exploded round them, then the whole age-old façade came crashing down.

3

I got a haircut. That was money I couldn't afford, but surely by now there'd be descriptions of me somewhere, on some Missing Persons file. I walked past a TV rental shop window and saw the News flickering on ten screens at once, and I didn't dare look, in case there was a photofit picture of me staring back. Sometimes a face in the crowd looked like Malcolm, and I felt my every muscle tensing, ready to break and run. And once I caught sight of a woman coming out of Mothercare, with a baby, and I quickly turned away, because she looked a bit like Mum.

I found an old fashioned barber's, none of your unisex stylists with the clever names, and told the man to make it really short. The woman at the squat, the one with the studs and pink hair, had offered to do it for me with the kitchen scissors. Get rid of those clothes as well, she'd said. She'd started to take an interest in me. 'So, you're AWOL,' she said.

'Pardon?'

'Absent Without Leave.' Now I looked, I reckoned she was older than my mum. It was only the hair and the gear that made you think she should be twenty. Her voice had a kind of a whine in it I couldn't take too much of, but when it came to the streetwise advice I took some notice. 'Get that hair cut. Get a bit of stubble on you, if you can.' I didn't like that 'If you can'. I *am* sixteen. Oh, and the clothes . . .

I came out of the Cancer Research shop in baggy blue

17

jeans and a nothing-much sweater. It all smelt old and it was hardly designer label stuff, but it fitted the bill. I was dressing for invisibility. I sneaked a look in a mirror-glass window on my way back, and just for a moment I didn't know who it was. I got Pinky a packet of Embassy on my way back, like she'd asked me to. When I got back to the house, she took them and didn't offer to pay.

There were somebody's friends of friends in the house, who'd been invited back after the first night's party, or that's what they said. No one bothered. Two of them had moved into my room; one was crashed out on my mattress, and the little hoard of bread and cheese I'd bought in for myself was gone. I found the guy with dreads and told him. 'Chill out,' he said, and I felt like lashing out at him. Like Malcolm had at me. 'Chill out,' he said again, still smiling but this time it felt like a warning.

Nights were worse. On the third night I got into the small room first and rammed the mattress up against the door. Some time past midnight there were people pushing at it, swearing vaguely. I pulled a cushion over my head, but didn't get much sleep. I kept on imagining that if I looked out . . . *really* slowly . . . there'd be the ceiling with the glow-stars on it, and Orion with his pin-man legs Dad gave him and size 13 feet.

Next morning I was feeling ragged, and the face that looked back from the mirror could have been the morning after quite some party, except nothing in this place so far had been any fun. I looked in my wallet—I kept it somewhere on me all the time now, day and night. Not a lot in there. Somehow I had to lay my hands on some money, and get out of here, and find a place of my own.

Baz's Basement Bar was not quite what I'd had in mind. Trouble was, when I asked about jobs at Kentucky Fried Chicken and any other name you've heard of, they would ask me for ID. I took a breath—be careful not to freeze now and look guilty. 'Sure,' I'd say, with hardly a second's hesitation, 'I'll just run home and get it.' Then I'd get out quick. Two or three of those in a half-mile radius, and I began to get paranoid. What if all their owners met up in the pub that evening, and happened to mention it? Some kid, going around all the places and he hasn't got ID. Would they call the police?

It was starting to get to me. Each time I asked I was thinking: just look normal. Make sure there's nothing about you they'll remember afterwards. But I felt myself going stiff and awkward, like when someone points a camera at you and says, 'Just look natural'. So I changed tack, headed for the back streets and eventually there was Baz's Basement Bar.

Baz was middle-aged, with a greasy look about him and a little thin moustache. He looked me up and down, quite slowly. 'I'll ask no questions,' he said slowly, and showed me to the kitchen sink. 'Good scrapings this side,' he said. 'Anything good for a curry. Anything with teeth marks, in the bin.'

'Uh . . . Aren't there regulations?' I said. 'Health and Safety?'

Baz's moustache became a tight black line. 'You want a job,' he said, 'or don't you? Oh, and you get paid a week in arrears.'

It was the end of the first week I went down with a gut ache. It was part of the perks, Baz said, that I could help myself to Friday night's left-over curry next day. Just before the evening shift it hit me, and I spent the night back at the house in the toilet, with the others barging and cursing at the door. Still, I struggled in to Baz's for lunchtime, feeling sore and ghostly. He met me at the door. 'So,' he grinned, 'you deigned to make it? Nothing good on TV? No good parties? Thought you might as well drop by?'

19

'Sorry,' I said.

'That was Saturday night,' he said. 'Only the busiest night of the week. Saturday nights is what I need someone like you for. Saturday nights,' he said slowly, 'is where your pay comes from. Got me?'

'Just a minute,' I said. 'That's not fair . . . '

'Fair,' Baz grinned, 'don't enter into the equation. I'll give you a tenner for the other nights. If you want to complain, well, just call the police.' His mouth widened slowly into a grin, then he laughed in my face.

On my way back, I passed them again, the Stone Saints. They were in the same pitch, just off the High Street, and this time there was a small crowd gathered round them, almost as still as they were. It was a mystery. I mean, what sort of show was this? If they'd been juggling or unicycling, something would have been happening, then it comes to an end and the people clap, and you come round with the hat. With human statues, people simply seemed to wait, and the longer they waited, the more they held their breath. It's hard to say what makes them reach into their pockets for a coin, just at the moment when they do, and turn away. It didn't make sense, and for some reason I wanted it to. Now I'd stopped, just like the others in the crowd, and I was staring. It was a mystery. There would be other mysteries, later, that I hadn't dreamed of yet.

The building must have been a church once, though it looked like some kind of offices now. There might never have been real statues in the niches, but the human ones were so right that the whole place could have been designed with them in mind. One of them had a monk's robe, the other had a bishop's mitre on his head, but they'd done the clothes so cleverly, with the same kind of gritty sand-coloured paint, that you couldn't see where the cloth ended and the human skin began. But that wasn't what brought me to a halt. It was their eyes.

You know how some old statues have those blank white eyes, so at first you think they're shut, then you realize they're open with nothing inside? The Saints' eyes weren't like that. There's a trick the ancient Greeks used, to make it look as if the eyes were watching you: they bored little holes where the pupils of the eyes would be. That's how the Saints' eyes looked, and it gave me a shudder. It was a moment before I realized that their eyes were shut, and the holes were painted, very neatly, on their eyelids. Just for that moment, though, I'd had a seasick feeling in the bottom of my stomach, and Baz's curry was only a part of it.

I was watching the eyelids now, and they were open just the slightest slit. I don't know how, but I knew they were aware of me—not me personally, maybe, but they'd be sensing the crowd, keeping an eye on the small change that plinked every now and then in the hat at their feet. There were notes in there too. As I watched, a Japanese man in suit and tie came up and stood between them; a camera went flash. The Saints didn't move an eyelid. There was a little ripple of applause from his colleagues, then they changed places, flash, and flash again. A little wad of notes dropped, neatly folded, in the hat.

This wasn't chickenfeed. You could live on that.

Then the clock struck—three bongs for the three-quarter hour—and the Saints began to move. They moved in small jerks, with a hand coming up, a head slightly turning, a foot stepping creakily down. They turned ninety degrees and faced each other with those borehole eyes. Click, clunk, they walked towards each other—not so much statues now but something automatic, and as creaky as if their joints were really sandstone. As they passed, one

/46,382

21

raised a hand to bless the other. They changed niches, and turned back to stone.

I watched till the hour, to see them move again. As it struck, a shocking thing happened: they stepped down and bowed to the people, just like in my dream. Then they opened their eyes and the strangeness was over; they turned to their lunch box, as if the rest of us had ceased to exist. The cluster of people broke up; in a minute there was no one still there watching them but me.

'Excuse me,' I said. No answer. I said it again.

One of the Saints turned with his mouth full of sandwich, took me in, shook his head. 'Please,' I said. 'I just want to . . .'

Both of them had rounded on me. 'Look,' said the second one, in an irritated little voice, 'we're off duty, OK? Come back in half an hour.'

'Please,' I said, 'I want to learn. Can you teach me?'

Both their looks went cold, as hard as when they had their statue-eyes. 'Beat it, kid,' said the first one. 'Run off home.'

I sat on a park bench, fuming. There was a statue, in mildewed bronze, of some man in a frock coat, looking out over the pond. Somehow he didn't look very impressive. I found myself noticing how he was standing, one leg slightly forward, one hand raised . . . like that. Anybody could do it. I found myself trying it, as I sat.

It was the *kid* that did it. There had to be an answer. Some stinging reply. But I knew I couldn't imagine it. They would just dismiss me, as they had done earlier. They'd turned their backs, and that was that.

But I'd say it another way, I'd show them. I wouldn't use words. And this time they wouldn't be able to turn their backs on me.

I went back to the charity shop. They didn't have what I wanted on the rails, but they had a big cardboard box full of unsorted stuff—50p any item, they said, though most of it's only good for fancy dress. When I'd found what I wanted, I slipped back to the house and shaved. I'd been proud of the stubble; it was coming on nicely, but this was important. Those two were going to talk to me, whether they liked it or not. This was going to be the crunch.

I waited till I was back there, in the little crowd around them, before I slipped on my stuff. I had the shorts on already, underneath my jeans. I was wearing the white shirt too; I looped the tie on, then the blazer and the old-fashioned Billy Bunter cap. Every bit of it was too small; it must have looked as if I was bursting at the seams, but that was OK. They'd notice. I squirmed to the front of the people, not far from the Stone Saints' feet, and sat.

Strange how it came back—that arms-and-legs-crossed posture everyone remembers from assemblies in primary school. Even that interested grin that we learn to please teachers, that looks as if you've looped some string between the corners of your mouth and ears and pulled. Grin, and keep it like that.

I froze. I was a statue too.

Even as a small kid, I could always do it. With a dull teacher, the others would mess about. They'd get told off in the end. Not me. I was good . . . except that I was too still and too quiet. I'd go rigid, not even blinking, till the teacher would start to feel uneasy. They'd get jittery, glancing around the room; they'd start forgetting words or dropping things. And they never knew why. Once, I told some of the others what I could do, and straight away they spoiled it, glancing at me and giggling, or trying to do it themselves. I soon realized this was a private thing. You did it in a public place, yes, the more public the better . . . but you did it alone.

23

My eyes were on the Saints. I didn't see their eyelids move one flicker, but I knew they'd seen me. Now that I couldn't look round either, I started to sense how it's done. You take your mind away from your straight-ahead vision—without moving your eyes or your focus, of course—and make yourself notice what's round the edge. Not much detail, naturally; what's there is kind of blurry, but you can see it, especially if it moves. I knew they'd be watching me the same way—maybe not when I sat down first, but they would now. As I sat, I realized how the crowd was fidgeting, shuffling, swaying back and forwards all the time, like wind in long grass. You've got to be really still yourself before you see it. What the Saints would see, at the edge of their vision, was my stillness. It would not be natural. They'd notice it and, like it or not, it would register: I was one of them.

The tourists and the shoppers felt it too. Without looking, I could feel a space clear back around me, as I became part of the show. The clock struck a quarter, and they did their changing-place routine. I stayed still. I could keep it up for longer than they could, I would show them. As they clicked back into their niches I realized my back was aching. Damn. I should have tried the posture out at home. If I could be just a bit more upright . . . But I couldn't move now. There was a twingeing up one side of my spine already, and for a crazy moment I thought: maybe they can sense that. Maybe when you're as still as they are you begin to take in things like that—a little glow, maybe, on the edge of the crowd where my back muscles were knotting into red-hot pain.

Their faces didn't move, but inside those stone masks, did I sense a smile? If I moved now, they still wouldn't quiver, but I'd be beaten and I'd walk away through the crowd with their silent and motionless laughter ringing in my ears.

My back felt like a knotted rope of aches now, but I sat. There was a swimming, sparkling feeling in my head; the ground was rocking slightly. But I sat.

Then the clock struck: *one . . . two . . . three . . .* Between each clang and the next it felt like a minute, but I held it: *six . . . and seven,* and the statues came alive, opened their eyes and smiled. There was a chinking of coins. The crowd dispersed.

After a minute or two, the one with the bishop's mitre came over and looked down at me. I tried to straighten a leg, but my knees had locked, and I winced with the pain of it. I tried to get to my feet, and came up with my back bent double like an old old man. Both of the statues were looking now, and laughing, then one of them held out a hand. 'Not bad, not bad,' he said, then the smile dropped. He narrowed his eyes. 'OK, kid, what do you want?'

4

The drop-in had the feeling of a church hall—trestle tables and a tea urn hissing in the serving hatch—and that's just what it was, tucked round at the back of St Jake's. Some of the regulars ignored the tables and sat on metal chairs around the outside, on their own and staring inwards, as if it was a long-stay hospital or station waiting room. Some of the faces had that vacant expression of people who don't expect anything to happen to them ever again. A few looked as if the drink or drugs had got to them badly over the years, but most had that nothingy look. 'If they'd just look you in the eye and *ask* . . . ' Mum used to say, when we'd ignored a beggar in the street. That was in the days when she used to feel guilty about these things—the days before Malcolm. 'Why do they have to mumble . . . ?' Maybe I could tell her now. When what you see mostly is knees going past and maybe one in a hundred passers-by shows any sign of hearing you, you go to a place inside your head and there you stay.

'No, it's not really our scene, either,' said the Saint who might have been the bishop. They were out of their gear now, with the paint smeared off their faces—though there was always a trace in the creases, any time I saw them, round the corners of their eyes. I couldn't guess which was which. They weren't twins—one was dark, one was fair—but the way they'd cut their hair, the way they sat and looked together, it was like a mirror image. I guessed they'd been together for a long time; maybe it was

26

like the way dog owners get to look like their dogs, or vice versa, who can say which?

'No, we're more the pavement café type. Cappuccino and a Danish pastry. But you've got to keep your nose to the ground. Keep au fait with the scene.' From the moment they had started talking to me I'd had a sinking feeling. These were not the awesome figures in my dream. The dream had woken me breathless, but it wasn't just fear. In that moment when the house came crashing down I'd been *excited*. As long as I got through the falling rubble without being flattened I'd be fine; I'd be free.

These two, though . . . They weren't the stuff that dreams are made on. Out in the street, it was their stillness that had been the scaring, thrilling thing.

'Are there other . . . entertainers, then?' I said. I could see a couple of battered guitar cases over by the window. There was even a small portable amp and folding keyboard.

'Us, we don't really belong,' said the first Saint. 'We're actors.' He paused meaningfully.

'Resting?' I said. I'd seen enough in my Young Stagers days to know that that's what actors mainly did.

'You call that *resting*?' the second one bridled. 'You try it!'

'I did,' I said. 'It hurt.'

'We're waiting,' said the first one. 'Waiting for the break. Films, that's where the money is.' They caught each other's eyes—a slightly desperate look, as if they'd heard each other say this many times before.

'We do a lot of work as extras. And the statuing . . . it's good for the technique.'

'The presence,' said the other, and he stared into his tea. In moments like this they went still, and both their faces fell into the same expression.

'Have you always been Saints?' I said.

27

'We came to it in stages,' said the fair one. 'We began as Tweedledum and Tweedledee.'

The dark one made a *pouf!* sound. 'Couldn't stand the fat stuff. All that padding. Imagine it, on hot days. Besides, the tourists didn't get the literary reference. With Saints, you're safe as houses in a place like this. It was Matty the Pan gave us the idea.'

'Ah, Matty the Pan,' sighed the other. 'There was a class act.'

'Was he a human statue too? Are there lots?'

'Lots? No. We're a select bunch. Matty was the tops, before he . . . ' There was the slightest hesitation. ' . . . went. Now there's the Tin Man—got a pitch near Starbuck's. Makes a play for the American tourists. All the Wizard of Oz fans, you see.'

'Maybe,' said the other, 'young Nick here should talk to Tin Man. He's, like, a career statue, not an actor, after all.'

The other nodded. 'Right. A lifelong occupation. Not like us.'

'Not like us,' chimed the other. 'We're just passing through.'

'Who's the boy? What's he after?' The Tin Man hardly raised his head, as if it was heavy to lift. It could have been a grand face, square-jawed, like one of those American telly-evangelists, but it showed its wear and tear. I thought of Mr Spangles, the children's entertainer who did all the birthday parties when I was at infant school. He dressed as a clown and he scared me, though I tried to laugh like all the others. He was too big, laughed too loudly, and had small disheartened eyes like the Tin Man's.

'I want to be a statue,' I said. 'I want to learn how it's done.'

28

There was a pause, as Tin Man lifted his big head and took in the Saints, decided not to speak to them, then turned to me. The Saints melted away, back to their table.

'Tweedledum and Tweedledee,' he said. 'Still what they are, as far as I'm concerned.' His words came in square blocks, as if chipped from stone. There was a long pause after each. 'Never lose your first character,' he said. 'Chances are, it's what you are.'

'You're the Tin Man?' I said. Every time he stopped talking, it felt as though he might never start again. To my surprise, he reached into an inner pocket and fished out a wallet of photographs. It was him, in some high street, in his shiny fake armour, stopped in the middle of walking.

'Pretty good, eh?' he said. 'I suppose you're too young to know the film.'

'He hasn't got a heart,' I said. 'The Yellow Brick Road.'

'Good, good.' He dealt another snapshot. In it he was holding up a heart, a rather convincing rubbery one, for all the crowd to see. 'Of course,' he said, 'I really need a video. Have you got a video?'

Laughing was the wrong thing to do. He stiffened, and the big hand on the table made a fist. 'Sorry,' I said. 'I mean . . . a video? Moving pictures?'

'Think about it. Anyone can be a statue in a photograph. They've got to *see* you not moving, haven't they?'

There was another of those pauses. 'They?' I said. 'Is there some kind of agency?'

He gave a quick glance round the room, and sideways at the two Saints. 'Tell you anything, did they? Tweedledum and Tweedledee? No? Well,' he relaxed. 'They wouldn't. They don't know a thing.'

'So there is an agency, then?'

'No. Or if there is, it's Mickey Mouse stuff. Want you

29

for some theme park, for Bank Holiday weekend. On the other hand . . . ' He leaned closer. 'Everybody knows about the . . . Watchers. They're sent.'

'Sent?' I said dimly. 'Who by?'

'Who? Who knows? If I knew that, I could go straight to them.'

'Watchers . . . ?' I said. There was something in his voice, the way he'd said it.

'Watchers,' he repeated. 'Don't mean tourists. Don't mean passers-by. The Watchers. First time you get one in your crowd, then you'll know what I mean.'

'What do they do?' I said.

He shook his head, as if it weighed a ton again. 'How should I know? Never approached me, yet. Not ready. If only I knew what it was, I'd do it better, but . . . ' He sat up, as if the interview was at an end.

'So what do I do?' I said.

'Character. Get one. You don't even know who you are.'

'Well?' said the dark Saint, when I got back to their table. I shrugged. For some reason I didn't want to mention the stuff about Watchers. It sounded crazy. Maybe something about the stillness did things to your head.

'Well?' said the fair one, and as I looked up at him I saw the door swing open, and there she was.

'Well?' they both said, but I wasn't listening. The girl had stepped in and paused for a moment, craning her long neck to scan round the room. She was probably pretty, but doing her best to hide it, with eyes narrowed in a frown and her lips in a scowl. She looked as young as me, and rather skinny, rather lost and pale, but if ever there was *presence*, that girl had it. She had come in without a sound, but I think everybody glanced up, even the ones who weren't quite there. Where people were talking away at a table, I'm prepared to bet there was a wingbeat's pause. Then everything was going on as normal. One of the Saints had waved her a small *Hi* of recognition, but the moment was over. The presence was gone. She was only a girl, a rather tired looking, maybe fed-up, girl. If she hadn't been wearing a ballerina's tutu, who'd have noticed her at all?

'God,' she muttered, as she came towards us. 'What an afternoon. I'm going to get this stuff off,' and she pushed on past towards the toilets.

'Who's that?' I said.

'Clockwork ballerina,' said the fair Saint. 'Swan Lake in slow motion.'

'Just a cygnet really,' said the other, 'but we call her Swan.' Their eyes met, for a silent boom-boom. 'I suppose you could talk to her.'

She was wearing rumpled jeans when she got back and her hair, which had been pulled back in a tight knot, tangled round her face. She slumped down at our table, shook her hair back, and she might have been a different girl.

'This is Nick,' said a Saint. 'He wants someone to teach him about statuing.'

I suppose I expected some kind of greeting at this point, at least a glance of recognition. She gave a little absent-minded *hnh* and looked over to the hatch. For some reason that annoyed me.

'Hi,' I said. 'What are you called when you're not called Swan?'

At last she turned to face me. She looked me up and down, sort of weary. 'You on a school project or something?' she said. That's when I realized I'd taken off the cap and blazer, but not the titchy school tie. I also noticed, close up, that she wasn't a kid. She was wiry and skinny, with the kind of build some girls have just as the

31

hormones get started, but she wasn't gawky or awkward; she was sure of herself, and twenty-something. Whether I was pleased or disappointed, I can't say.

'I'm serious,' I said. 'I need to do something—I mean, really need to. I think I could do this.'

'Don't,' she said. Her eyes, now she was looking at me straight, were a very pale grey. 'Where are you from?'

'Not round here.'

'Uh-huh. Got a roof over your head?'

'Only just. I've got to do something.'

'Beg,' she said. It wasn't exactly a smile that crossed her face, but it had softened. She noticed my reaction, too. 'Don't worry,' she said, 'it's quite normal nowadays. You make more money. There's no future in this.' She began to turn away.

'That's not what the Tin Man said. He seemed to think there were . . . openings.' She had looked back now; her eyes narrowed. 'He said there were talent scouts out there. He said Watchers . . .'

'Yeah, well,' she said sharply. 'That just shows how it gets you, this game. You go funny in the head.' Our eyes met. I didn't say: what about you, then? She shook her head slowly, as if the tiredness had caught up with her again. 'Go home,' she said. 'Whatever it's like, it can't be worse.'

'It can,' I said.

'That's what you think. At least . . .' she said and laid a hand on my arm. She could have been an older sister. 'At least promise me. You'll give it one more try. Just so you're really sure.'

On the way back to the squat I stepped into a phone booth, and I stood there for a long time, my hand on the set. I picked up the receiver, hesitating till the phone went

32

Beeeeee. Start again. I dialled. She could be right. What if I was making up a story, after all? Maybe the booby-trap thing with the garage hadn't even worked. Or it had, and it had done the trick. I liked that idea better. I could see Malcolm blazing, I could see him crashing round the house, saying, '*I'll kill him. I'll break the little bleeder's neck.*'

Halfway through dialling, I stopped. I pressed New Call, and punched in the 171 code, to withhold the number, just in case, and dialled again.

Yes, I imagined Malcolm storming, raging, then . . . And then—slow motion on this bit, and the camera swivels round to close-up on her face—Mum would come to her senses. Mum's got a nice face, really, when she smiles at you, and now I could visualize the moment as a light went on inside her eyes and the soppy I-love-Malcolm look dropped away and she saw what the man was really like. Maybe all she would say at first was 'It's only a car, for God's sake,' but he'd go berserk at that, maybe even raise his fist to her, too. Then it would all be crystal clear to her—what was worth more, her son or that car? Any second she'd pick up the phone now and she'd say, 'Thank God, I've been so worried. Come home . . . '

It rang. It rang again. I held my breath. It was going to be all right. It rang three, four times, then a click. An answerphone. We'd never had an answerphone. What did I do now? What could I say?

Next moment the voice clicked on, and all the questions fell away. The voice was Malcolm's. He'd moved in; there was his voice, there were their names together, and not a mention of mine, for all the world to hear.

5

*M*um. This is Nick. Your son, remember? Well, you can forget now, 'cause I'm fine, just fine. And you can tell that bastard Malcolm . . .

No, no. Take a breath and start again.

Hi, Mum. Look, I'm sorry. But you mustn't worry. I've got a job and a place to live; I'll be OK. Oh, and tell Malcolm I'm sorry about the car. You do understand, don't you? Love you. Bye.

My throat went dry. This wasn't the real thing, of course. I was standing in the phone box holding the phone but I wasn't connected. This was a dummy run, the fifth or sixth, in fact. When I'd dialled earlier and heard Malcolm's voice on the answerphone I'd slammed the handset down and held it in place, my heart thumping. Would there be a click? Would they, somehow, know? Next time I mustn't panic. I'd stood for five minutes with a feeling like a cold wind in my head. Then there'd been a knock on the glass—a couple of girls outside, giggling. Sorry, I said, and let them go first. They were ages, hooting with laughter, passing the phone back and forth, and every now and then they glanced outside to see if I was still there, and giggled again.

When I got back inside, I took a deep breath. Insert Coins, the display flashed. I picked up the handset, clutching it too tight, and rehearsed it out loud again, first one way then another. I never got to *Love you. Bye.* It was no good. In my mind's eye I could see the hall at home, and Malcolm, smirking, as my tinny little voice played back from the machine, sounding hollow and small and very far away.

Besides, don't chance it. Even if I withheld the number, mightn't there be ways the police could trace it? I didn't know. Why don't they teach you useful things like that at school?

No, best to leave it. As I strode home in the streetlight I was feeling empty, as if I'd gone for an audition and never been called. There were words rattling round in my head. *See?* I was muttering. *You see what I mean? Now do you believe me?*

Who was I trying to convince? It felt like an argument, though I couldn't hear the answers. Who was I talking to?

Not Mum, not Malcolm, not myself. With a little shock I realized I was talking to Swan.

She was a class act. She was very good indeed. It was ten in the morning, and I'd trawled the tourist bits of town, asking passers-by, until I found her, in a shopping precinct. There was an ornamental pond behind her. I smiled, and guessed she'd planned that: Swan, with Lake . . . Swan herself, she'd changed again—not the street kid in jeans, not the gawky girl late home from ballet class, not even the grey-eyed elder sister. At first I thought it was a plaster model of her, she was so white and so still. From the girl I'd seen in the drop-in, with the face that changed expression every minute, she'd changed into a ballerina doll.

White tights, white tutu, and white ballet shoes: she was white all over, not her natural pale but a complete white-out of stage paint on her face and neck and bare arms. The only black was the box, like a tiny stage, she stood on, and her hair and eyebrows, as slick as sucked

35

liquorice. Her lips were a pout of artificial scarlet, though I could see the real line of her mouth beneath it, thin with concentration. When she stretched her arms above her head there was a place in the armpit where the paint had wrinkled slightly, just where she must shave. I looked away as though I'd spied into a private place.

I guessed that she knew I was watching her, the way the Saints knew yesterday. There were always a handful of people looking on. They came and went; I stayed. Watching. I thought of the Tin Man in the drop-in, and the way he'd said it: *There are Watchers*. What were Watchers? Swan and the Saints had shrugged when I mentioned the word: the Tin Man was odd in the head. But they shrugged too hard and talked too fast, not looking at me, so I knew: yes, they knew what I meant.

Had I become a Watcher now?

There was a click. From a box by her feet, a thin tinkling tune struck up and she moved, with slow jerks, from one position to another. She was clockwork, a toy ballerina on an old-fashioned musical box. The mechanical movements made her even less flesh-and-blood than stillness did. In some of the postures, up on points, I could see the slight trembling and the muscles of her calves were taut as wires. Pure control.

Go home, she had said. Well, I'd done what I could: I'd picked up that phone last night. And home, home as I'd known it, wasn't there any more. Why I wanted her to know that, I couldn't have told you. It just mattered, that's all. And she was good—still as stone, up on points, for minutes on end, then her arms would move or she would swivel in the slowest pirouette. She would click into a slow bow, and the coins came tinkling at her feet. It was when she was still, though, that the strangeness of it hit me. I suddenly saw how vulnerable you were, standing in public. Up on points again, stopped, without even the

36

music, she looked fragile, however tough she talked. Anyone could come and stare, as if they owned her; anyone could laugh at her, or fall in love with her, or worse.

Then I sensed it: I wasn't the only one in the crowd who'd been here watching all this time. I was picking up that instinct, the way when you're still you can spot stillness in the ebb and flow of people, and suddenly I knew there was someone else, another odd one out . . . only I didn't know yet who it was. I'd been fixed on Swan. Now I let my eyes take in the people round me, let everything blur a little, and watched for who was moving, and who not. The crowd became a sort of liquid, with swirls of colour in it, as people's holiday shirts and T-shirt logos and sunhats came and went. Just beyond, there was a patch of grey, and stillness. I blinked into focus again, and at first I'd lost it; then a bunch of French kids shifted and there he was, right at the back of the crowd, in the shadow of a tree. He wore a baggy grey bomber jacket, zipped right up even in the heat, and tight grey jeans. It wasn't the style you'd expect on a man so old. His face was the colour of ash, and deeply lined—not laughter lines, but a criss-cross of wrinkles that gave his face a beat-up, ravaged look. He was thin, and still tall, though stooping slightly, and I had the image of a heron, an old grey bird motionless above the water with its rusty dagger beak.

I must have stared, or maybe he was equipped with the same kind of instinct I was learning, because almost the second my eyes rested on him, he turned his head and looked at me. For a moment I couldn't breathe, as if I'd jumped into cold water. Since I'd been on the run nobody, not even Swan last night, had looked at me like that. I could say it was like a searchlight, picking me out in the crowd, except that there was nothing light about it.

Imagine a beam not of light but of dark, so concentrated that it dazzles you; you have to look away.

And when I blinked and looked back, he was gone.

Half an hour later I was trying to work out what I'd done wrong. Swan should have been grateful when I told her about the grey man. I mean, he looked like a creep, a dirty old man, and I'd wanted to warn her. 'I was worried about you,' was what I meant, though I don't think I knew it myself, not yet. The way I imagined it, she'd be grateful, and she'd smile and relax, and I'd say, 'How about a cup of coffee,' and we'd talk after that.

I was wrong. I waited half an hour before she took a break. As she bent down to scoop up the small change, she looked suddenly young and pale again. 'Hi,' I said, as if I'd just happened by, and then I told her. As I spoke, her eyes went very cold. Through the white paint, close-up, I saw little creases of anger between the painted eyebrows and around the lipstick mouth.

'What business of yours is it?' She was speaking quietly, but sharp. Then her face changed again. Just for a moment it looked almost pleading. 'Which way did he go?'

'I don't know. He was under the tree, and then he'd vanished.'

She turned away abruptly, busy with her black box. 'Sorry,' I said. Half an hour ago the man in grey had spooked me slightly. Now I'd told her; she'd been disappointed, and that spooked me more. 'Sorry,' I said, 'I just thought . . .'

'Don't,' she sighed. 'If you want to try this business, if you *really* want to . . . try it. But not on my patch, understand? Not here.'

As I came round the end of the street I noticed that something had changed. In the garden of the squat, the wheelie bin had been set upright, though the contents were still trodden in the dust. Next to it was a new blue notice on a short pole hammered in the ground. Homepride Estate Agents, it said, and the words SOLD BY very big and blue.

I banged on the door for some time. Just as I was starting to think, *that's it, everybody's up and gone*, the window opened just a crack and Dreads looked out. 'Siege time,' he said, when he'd hustled me in. 'We've got a day or two, I reckon, then they'll send the pigs, if we're lucky.'

'The police?' I said, a bit too sharply.

'No prob. All they can do is serve notice. I know the form.' He looked at me. 'Hey, you're really worried, aren't you? What've you done? OK, don't tell me. Point is, they might send the bailiffs in instead. Those guys are trouble.'

'What'll you do?' I said.

'Some of the people here, they reckon they're up for a fight. Matter of principle. Me, I'm not keen on blokes with crowbars. You can stay if you like.'

Upstairs it looked as if most of last night's crowd had voted with their feet. Someone had ripped open a mattress, for some reason, and its lumpy stuffing spilled out on the floor. I found my bag of spare clothes where I'd hidden it, at the back of the airing cupboard. A day or two, he'd said. Now I had to do something. One way or another, this hiding place was coming to an end.

I wandered round the upstairs rooms, all empty now, and all of a sudden I felt sad. You could see from the wallpaper this had been a family home once. In the small room at the back there were Disney characters all over the wall. People had felt-penned slogans round them, and a few dirty comments, and the circle-A for Anarchy. I opened the little cupboard in the eaves and there was still part of an old cot in there, and a Barbie doll in a frilly short skirt, without one arm. The other one was raised, though, in a way that made me think of Swan. At the back of the cupboard was a white plastic recorder. I picked it up and tried it; years of music lessons, the kind your parents think are good for you but can never explain quite why, came flooding back, and I remembered old Miss Augustine, the music teacher, who always smelt slightly of sherry. My fingers started tracing the shapes for the cleverest thing I'd learned, a simple piece of Bach. That's when I knew, and I shook off the sad feeling like a wet dog shakes off water. I was going to be a statue, for real, and I knew what kind of statue I would be.

The exact kit was more of a problem, but I had a feeling that I'd seen the answer somewhere. One of the charity shops, in the fancy-dress box . . . I couldn't remember which. It was at the fourth or fifth attempt I got it—yes, and there it was, a sort of cream-white jacket with lots of braid on the front, the kind you see Mozart wearing in schoolbook pictures of him as a kid.

'How much?' I said, trying to sound cool, in case I sounded too keen and the price went up.

'Oh.' The woman scarcely glanced. 'A couple of quid.'

Finding the knickerbockers was a problem, but there were some knee-length things on the women's rail that would just about do. Then I rooted round in the women's socks and knickers box and found the right colour tights. 'Fancy-dress party,' I muttered as I gave the woman 50p.

'Hmph,' she said. When I asked her where I could get the eighteenth century wig to go with the outfit, she began to believe me. 'Funny you should say that,' she said. 'We

40

did a house clearance last week, and the old bloke must have been a barrister or summat. Nasty horsehair article, but you can try it if you like.'

It was getting the face paint from the theatrical hire shop that nearly broke me. Afterwards I counted out what I had left. No way enough to feed me, let alone to get a proper rented room. However tatty it was, they would ask me to put down a deposit. I needed to be making money now, and fast.

Next stop, I made my way to Starbuck's. There was the Tin Man, holding up his heart. He was still enough, but I wasn't that impressed. Under his tin-plate armour and hat, there was nothing of him showing but his face. He might as well really be a statue, I thought, sniffily. When something clinked in his hat, he started walking, robot-fashion, on the spot. It was dull. I knew who I was comparing him to: Swan. Now, she was *good*.

When I'd practised, when I'd got the hang of this game, I'd want Swan to know about it.

'Tin Man,' I whispered, when he took a breather. 'Look, I've got my gear.' His eyes, among the metal make-up, gave a glitter of alarm. 'It's OK,' I said. 'Not here. Where can I go that isn't anybody's pitch?'

He relaxed. 'What are you?' he said.

'Sort of Mozart,' I said.

'Sort of?' he snorted. 'Huh! Music, though. How about the bandstand, Ewart Park?'

'Thanks,' I said then, as he was turning away, 'I think I saw one. A Watcher.' I described the grey man as well as I could. As I spoke I saw the Tin Man's hands clenching.

'Him,' he said. 'Him! He's back!' Then he was shaking his head, and whatever I said he simply turned away from me. He stepped back to his pitch and became a statue, without another word.

41

6

Once long ago, in a life not much like this one, I was the kind of friend who's usually up for it: whatever the others were trying I'd try once, at least. No big confessions, though . . . I'm thinking about the time some of our crowd got into Live Role Play—you know, when you dress up as warriors and goblins and run around in the woods. There was meant to be some serious battle-gaming in it—cunning strategy and that—but as far as I could see this was dressing up, the kind you do when you're six or seven, except we got to do it out of doors and after dark and without anybody's mum or dad looking on. Fine by me—it was a laugh, as long as we stayed deep in the woods and no one except other idiots in hobbit costumes got to see me.

And here I was now, deep in a thicket in my Mozart costume. Dressing up. The hitch was that there was no one around to share the game with, and in a moment I was going to walk out of the bushes, walk to the most public place I dared, so anyone who liked could come and stare at me.

I'd come to the furthest corner of the park, off the main paths; the gardeners had given up and let the bushes go wild and tangled, but there were a few small clearings you could reach if you didn't mind brambles. No way could anyone just happen to pass by. I was out of sight and, I hoped, out of earshot. Still, when I put the recorder to my lips and tried a few notes, I felt like a small kid in front of the class for the first time at school. Gradually it came, though, my only bit of Mozart—the main tune from 'Eine Kleine Nachtmusik', the one everybody recognizes even if they don't know what it's called. On the third or fourth try, I got right the way through. Now I had to do it again, with the movement—or rather the stillness, first of all. I was a plaster statue of young Mozart, poised with my fingers on the holes of the recorder. Then the trick I'd learned from watching Swan, the puppet-ballerina. I'd wait for the sound of a coin in the box at my feet. When it came at last, like the clunk of a slot machine, I'd jerk into motion, very slowly, as if there were cogs and gears inside me bringing the recorder up to my lips, and slowly play the first notes, warming up gradually to normal speed . . . then slowing down, running out of steam. Someone would put another 10p in, they'd have to, just to hear the end of it.

It sounded simple, put like that. Standing alone in the undergrowth, in a smell of mud and wet leaves, it felt stupid. Then I thought of Swan, and the looks on the faces of the people watching. I was nothing like her, but what about the Tin Man? People stopped and gave him money. A bit of practice and I could be more interesting than him.

Then a twig cracked somewhere, and I jumped. The tune died with a squeak and I looked round, my heart beating fast. I froze as the bushes crashed open and out bounded a long tall dog, a Dalmatian. It rushed at me, skidded to a halt, lolled out its tongue, flopped twice around in circles then crashed back into the foliage. Everything was quiet again. I raised the recorder to my lips, but I was shaking. It wouldn't stay still.

The grey Watcher: I could see him in my mind now, silent and motionless, like when I'd watched him watching Swan. He wouldn't rustle the leaves or make a twig crack. If he'd been in hiding, watching me, I'd never know.

43

Suddenly I wanted to be in the bandstand. At least there'd be people. I didn't care about practising. Whatever the Saints might say to fob me off, I knew there was a Watcher in town, and he'd seen me. I just knew I didn't want to be alone.

When I got to the bandstand, there was no one there. I found my spot and started standing. I didn't do badly, I thought, but what was the point? A small gang of kids came by and sniggered, but they didn't stop. Now and then there was a jogger but they didn't even slacken speed. Then I thought of the Tin Man and it made me want to spit with anger. He knew what he was doing. He'd sent me to a lousy useless pitch, and he'd done it on purpose. Pretty stupid of me not to realize that neither he nor anyone else was going to help me: we were rivals, after all. He just wanted me out of the way.

I gathered up my stuff and set out looking. It wasn't what I'd planned, to be trailing through town in my costume, and I drew a few looks as I went. It was lucky I was angry, or I'd have folded with embarrassment. Wearing the Mozart clothes and white face paint on a pitch, with an audience, was one thing, but just walking around in it . . . ? No.

Then there was an alley that cut round the back of the Abbey. One end was almost blocked by the cream and brown awning of a coffee stall. Beyond that it widened, and there was a steady trickle of tourists wandering through.

The coffee smelt great, too. Irresistible. I hadn't had a real one for days.

As I took my cardboard cup, I saw the guy on the stall was kind of smiling. He didn't look like a serious career coffee vendor—more like a student earning a bit on the side. He wasn't much older than me. 'Can I go there?' I said, nodding at the alley. 'Is it anyone's pitch?'

'Don't think so,' he said. 'You got a licence?'

'Licence?'

'Uh-oh,' he said. 'I see. I think you apply to the council; they give you a permit. They don't want just any old buskers. They want proper acts on the street.' He must have seen the look on my face through the paint. The Tin Man hadn't mentioned this stuff either. Maybe he hoped that I'd just get arrested. Neat.

And what would happen then? They'd want to know my name, and my age, and where I came from, and that would be the end of that, for sure.

'Tell you what,' said the guy on the coffee stall. 'If I see a cop coming, I'll give you a shout.' He gave me a grin, and just for a moment I seemed to remember a world where people were mates, and smiled and did each other favours. 'Then,' he said, 'statue or no statue, better move on quick.'

I could do it. I might not be great but I could do it. I got the shakes in my hand from muscle strain, but I got to know how you shift the weight or your posture, very slightly, gradually, so no one sees. There was a moment of panic when a cramp shot down my leg and I thought: that's it, I'll be writhing on the pavement in a minute, but I willed and willed the muscle to relax, relax, and concentrated on my breathing, and it did, it did. And the people came by; most of them only stopped a minute, because there's only so much stillness you can stand. Then some of them, a few, enough, would dig into their pockets. As the hours went by, I thought that I might learn to know in advance which ones they'd be. With each clink in the box, the careful jerking of my clockwork got neater and the music came out with a few, but not too many, squeaks.

45

Around lunchtime, I went into a burger bar round the corner. I knew I should be saving up the takings, eking it out carefully, but today was a first, a kind of celebration, so I got the biggest on the menu and I ate.

It was halfway through the afternoon, back in the alley, that the boredom hit me. Up till then, I'd needed every gram of my attention on the stillness, or the music, or wondering what I'd do if some kid made a grab for my money. From about four o'clock, I realized I was on a kind of auto-pilot, and for the first time I let my mind drift.

The voice on the answerphone. Malcolm. Mum, and . . . What would it be like, this baby, half my mum, half Malcolm? No, don't think about it. Try not to think at all. But it was too late now: my mind had started.

Mum had friends. What if one of them just happened by—on holiday, on a shopping expedition? Or what if it wasn't the police who checked up on street licences, but some plain-clothes inspector, so you couldn't spot the uniform? What if one of them was sneaking down the alleyway behind me now?

And the Watcher . . . ?

As I thought the word, I might have jerked a little, like you do in class on the day after a good party when you nod and snap back from a doze. I stiffened. Watch it. Had I dozed off, had I started nodding? There were half a dozen people looking but I couldn't guess what they'd seen. No boos and hisses anyway. Maybe it was good sport to watch a statue falling asleep on the job.

Then suddenly I knew that *he* was somewhere, watching. There was a greyness, a cold deep kind of greyness, out on the edge of my vision, in a place I could only feel, not see. Of course, I thought, he'd know what he was doing. He's not some common-or-garden weirdo; he knows this game and he knows what a statue can see. He was over to my left, where the shadow of the Abbey fell, and I could feel his gaze like a cold draught on that side of my face.

Someone emptied a purseful of tiny change into my box, and what could I do? I click-click-clicked into my Mozart for the twentieth time that afternoon.

A little later I wondered whether I had been wrong. The sky above had clouded over, dirty dishcloth grey. Maybe it had really been a cold wind, and I was imagining the grey man. I nearly smiled as the first big drops fell. Then everyone was scurrying out of the rain; my little crowd dissolved. I started gathering up my things.

As I turned to the end of the alley, away from the High Street, I saw that I hadn't been wrong. He was there.

He was standing in the middle of the alleyway, taking no notice of the rain. I could see it splashing on his head, which had a high bald patch among the thin and straggly grey hair. His face was glistening with it, but he never blinked or moved his stare. I turned to go, but tripped over my box and sent the coins scattering. As I bent down to scoop them up from the wet stones, he was there behind me, without a sound, looking down. He spoke.

At first I didn't catch the words—just a jumble of sounds. Then I recognized the lilt of an accent. It might have been French, but there was a harsher edge to it than that. 'You have it,' he said, slowly, twice. 'You have it.'

'Who are you?' I said.

He had a way about him that I'd learn to recognize, later: he seemed not to hear what you'd said. The next line might actually be an answer but he'd say it as if he was reading from a script he'd written in advance. I caught a whiff of a smell about him, that might have been years of bad tobacco; it was bitter and stale.

'No technique,' he said. 'Quite remarkable. Absolutely none. It should be *merde*, your performance. And yet I see you have it. It! I will make you an offer.'

47

'Offer?' I repeated, still feeling about for scattered 1p pieces. He put the toe of a long suede shoe, a rather elegant shoe, against my box and flicked it hard, so the coins sprayed out again. 'Hey . . . !'

'Leave it,' he said sharply. 'This is nothing. Nothing. Come with me. Soon you will laugh at this peedling small change. You will *laugh*!' The last word was a bark, a cough, so loud that I staggered backwards. I was on my feet, with my bag in my hand, and I didn't look back for the small change; I just turned and ran.

Why did I do that? Tell me, why?

I was staring in the mirror, above a basin full of white scummed froth. It was one of those toilets with a low turnstile that you're tempted to vault over, except there's a one-way mirror and an attendant who might just be watching. This time I paid my 20p meekly; I was going to use every facility they had. There hadn't been any hot water in the squat for several days, and I wanted the white paint scrubbed off every inch of me. I didn't want tell-tale white in the creases, either, like I'd seen on other statues. If I passed the grey man in the street now, I wanted to think he wouldn't recognize me.

But why? my own face asked me. What was so bad about what happened? Now I played it back in my mind, was I such a kid that I'd been rattled by a foreign accent? What was so wrong with what he'd said?

You have it. He wanted to make me an offer. Didn't I want a break, didn't I need one, and pretty damn quick? The bailiffs could be banging on the door of the squat any day now; I'd be on the street. I'd seen them, in shop doorways—the really homeless kids, with that awful empty see-through look and their mouths on automatic: *Spare some change?* Everyone needed the big break—the Tin

48

Man, Swan, the Stone Saints—and wasn't this it, the offer they would kill for? At least I could have talked to him, and sussed out the deal?

Maybe Swan had been right, the way she'd looked at me in the drop-in. I could see what she thought: that I was a kid in a sulk, playing runaway. Dressing up. If she saw me now, what would she say?

I went back to the alleyway. I admit it: I slunk back, as if by some wild chance he might still be there waiting. He wasn't, of course. I tried the Tin Man's pitch, standing back out of sight, in case the grey man was watching him. No. I passed the Saints, then went to Swan's pitch. No one there at all. I felt a twinge: if there was anyone I'd tell about this, it was her. I needed to talk to somebody, and not just anybody: Swan. I cut back to the drop-in and got through several mugs of coffee, till it started to give me the jitters. I was gearing myself up. When Swan came in, any time now, I would tell her. Even if she laughed out loud, I wouldn't care.

'You will laugh at this,' echoed the voice in my head. The Grey Man. 'You will *laugh*!' I shuddered, as if he could somehow be inside my mind, still watching. The memory seemed to shatter into laughter, though that afternoon he'd watched my stumbling stupid exit silently.

Another hour, and Swan was still not there. Instead, the Saints arrived. I avoided their eyes and stared into my coffee. A bit later I heard the Tin Man's voice, sharp and rising: '*You* saw him . . . !' I looked up and saw he was talking to me.

'You said you saw him,' said the Tin Man. 'Tell them what he looked like.' There was an edge in his voice that could have been anger or fear.

'Was he kind of tall?' said the fair Saint. 'Grey hair?' said the other. 'Sort of down to his neck like this . . . ? What was he wearing?' As I told them, the Stone Saints nodded to each other. 'Yup,' they said to Tin Man. 'That was the one we saw her with.'

'Who . . . ?' I said, and my voice had an echoey feel.

'This man,' they said together. 'The one you saw.'

'I mean: who . . . ?' Somehow none of my words would come out right. 'Her? Who . . . ?'

'Swan, of course . . .'

Then the Tin Man broke down. 'Christ!' he shouted, and everybody in the drop-in, however glazed or exhausted, lifted up their heads and looked at him. 'Her! That ugly, skinny . . . little . . . punk!' He lifted a water glass high in his fist. 'I've got twenty years' experience, and did he look at me? I'm the Tin Man, look, the Tin Man . . . ' And he squeezed the glass as if his hand was really made of metal—squeezed until the sweat drops came out on his forehead—squeezed and . . . crack, the glass splintered. The last of the water in it trickled down his arm, going gradually pink with his blood.

One of the elderly buskers was looking over. 'Ye mark m' words,' he said, and he tapped his long nose. 'That's the last ye'll see of her.' He turned back to his table, as if there was somebody with him. 'Mark m' words,' he nodded sagely to the thin air. 'That's the last *anyone* will *ever* see of her!'

7

I banged on the door. There was something different
in the sound it made. When there was no answer I
tried the side gate; ever since I'd been in the squat the
back window had been hanging open. But the gate was
locked, with a new brass lock that hadn't been there
before. Now I looked at the front door, there was a glint of
new brass there too. All the locks had been changed.

I banged again. 'Hey,' I shouted up at the window,
where Dreads's head was bound to poke out in a moment.
He seemed to spend most of his life in that room, smoking
or sleeping or swaying to his headphones, in another
world. If not him, the pink-haired woman would hear me,
or one of the others. They'd got organized, obviously; they
were getting ready for a siege. 'Hey,' I called again, 'it's
me.'

A window slammed up—not in the squat but next
door, and the head and shoulders that appeared were a
middle-aged man's. 'Stop that shouting,' he said. 'If you
want your little friends, they've gone.'

'Gone?'

'Gone and good riddance. You, too. We've had enough
of you scum round here. And don't even think of it . . . '
I was thinking of my bag of spare clothes and my wash
kit, upstairs in the cupboard; I must have glanced at the
window. 'Touch that window and I'll be on to the police.
It's breaking and entering, you know. I've got a phone
here. Clear off!'

That's when I noticed that his voice was trembling. He

wasn't just angry; he was afraid. I didn't know what it was he saw when he looked at me. Gangs of crack dealers? Anarchy? His street becoming a slum? Everything he'd worked for going down the plughole? Suddenly the world seemed very bleak, and sort of lonely, as the window slammed. His small grey face was in the window, watching, as I walked away.

I went back to the drop-in. Where else was there? I had to speak to someone, someone who recognized my face at least, before I could think what to do. I counted the money I'd got left and I swore at myself. If it hadn't been for that moment of panic in the alley, if it hadn't been for the burger at lunchtime, I might have had enough to find somewhere, for one night's B & B.

The Saints and the Tin Man were gone. There was no one in the place I recognized, except the ancient busker with the long nose. He was still chatting indistinctly to some invisible friend. I went over and waited for him to look up. He didn't. 'Excuse me,' I said.

'Why?' He looked up sidelong. 'What have you done?' Then he turned to the empty chair facing him and laughed at the joke.

'Where do people go for the night,' I said, 'when . . . when they haven't got anywhere?'

He looked me up and down, not laughing. 'You got *any* money?' he said. 'Any at all?'

I nodded. 'A bit.'

'Well, give me a quid and I'll give you good advice,' he said. I hesitated. 'Take it or leave it,' he said.

'OK.' I slapped the coin on the table. His hand shot out but mine was faster. As I slapped my hand on the pound, his hand clamped down on mine; it felt like wood. The smell of him hit me, sour cider. 'Only if the advice is

52

any use,' I said, as steady as I could. Our eyes met. Among the folds of lids and the yellowing and bloodshot, his eyes were almost colourless. Be a statue, I thought. Don't look away. He'll have you if you blink.

Then suddenly his eyes creased and he laughed. 'Smart kid,' he said. 'Don't push y' luck, though.'

'What's the good advice?' I said.

'Never lay y' money down before you got the goods!' He had a little chortle. 'But here's a tad more, free o' charge. Don't do doorways or parks. It's tourist season, see? The cops want the streets nice and tidy. Don't chance the night shelter, neither. You think you're canny but they'll eat you alive. You got ten quid? Place called Henderson's Hotel.' He smirked at the man who wasn't there, then turned back, straight. 'Go there,' he said. 'Keep the quid if you got to. And in the morning, bugger off home, there's a good lad.'

'Hotel' wasn't the word I'd have used for Henderson's. It was tucked at the back of a multi-storey car park, with a boarded-up shop next door. It had some brown paint left, and swags of greyish lace in the windows, but the place had a fortified look. There were a couple of locks on the steel-panelled door. I rang, and a door phone crackled. 'A room,' I shouted into it. No answer. It buzzed slightly. 'I want a room for the night.' There was a long pause, then a slot in the door clacked open. Inside, there was a wire grille, and behind that a pair of watchful eyes. I stood in the light, so they could see me. When the door opened, just a crack, there was a smell like Great-Aunt Kath's house had, one awful visit, not long before she went into a home. I'd been five, and I'd run for the door and started crying; Mum brought me back, holding my hand very tight, but I kept gasping. 'Don't be silly,' she said, shaking me, then, 'Don't be so rude.' I was trying to hold my breath till we got home.

I didn't sleep much in Henderson's. The man took my money before he let me step off the doormat then, as if he still had his doubts, led me upstairs. I was on the third floor at the back, in a room that was half a room—I could see where the hardboard wall had been slapped up, with a crack around the edge. I shut the door and clicked down the latch, then I lay on the hard bed. I kept my clothes on. The sheets weren't exactly dirty but there was something about them that I didn't want to touch. All at once the memory of soft sheets and a duvet, the smell and the touch of them, swept back over me, and if there'd been a soft pillow I'd have sunk my face in it and cried.

But I wasn't going to think about that. If I did, I would really start losing it. I knew I was that close. I might panic, run out in the streets and start hitch-hiking, or flag down a passing police car and say: I give up; take me home. No, I mustn't think that. There wasn't a place called *home*, with Malcolm. I mustn't think at all. My stomach creaked. I was starting to be hungry, but I mustn't think about that either. There would be a breakfast . . . how many hours off? I mustn't start counting. I must try to get some sleep.

Three hours later, I was stiff with the effort of trying. I had lumped the pillow up around my ears, but it made no difference. There was one voice shouting, off and on and suddenly, in the room upstairs. On my own floor, the third, there were snores, and later, a woman's voice weeping for a while. Once, downstairs in the hallway, there was a sound like a scuffle, but no voices, just a sound of breaths and heavy bumping, until other voices started shouting at them to shut it or they'd come and sort them both out. I lay on my iron cot bed and tried not to think that the toilet was a floor and a half down, on the

54

turn of the stair. I tried not to need it, but the more I thought the more I did, and lay there till my bladder ached.

I stared at the ceiling. I wished there were glow stars now.

The morning came early. I looked out of the narrow window, out past the multi-storey to the railway sidings, and some cracks of light were creeping in among a dirty sky. It was going to rain again, and I knew what that meant. No one goes strolling, stopping to amuse themselves with human statues, in the rain.

Then breakfast, and I would have eaten anything. I kept my eyes down on the streaky bacon. No one talked: it was quieter than it had been all night. I had my carrier bag of Mozart clothes with me, on the floor between my feet. I didn't want to look around the other faces and guess which one had been shouting, which one weeping, which ones scuffling on the stairs. When I did glance up, I noticed that no one else looked at each other either. One man was staring round, but blankly, and his gaze passed over me as if he didn't see.

Nine o'clock, we were turned out, everyone, and no returns till six. I heard someone shouting upstairs as the cleaner flushed him out and sent him downstairs, clattering his bucket and broom. And the weird thing was that I didn't feel bad. There'd been a moment in the night when I could have cut and run; now, with tea and bacon and some flabby white bread in my stomach, the world looked possible after all.

As the other residents emerged on the pavement they would stop and look around. What now? they seemed to say. Well, I wouldn't be one of them. I was going to stride out, straight for the High Street, like a man with somewhere else to go to. I'd survived a bad night, and it was a new day. I took a breath and strode.

I got as far as the opposite pavement when the woman stepped out in front of me. I moved to one side, but she moved too, blocking my way.

'Excuse me,' she said. 'Can I have a word with you?' If this had been a shopping precinct, she'd have been one of those market research people with a clipboard and a questionnaire, and I was about to shake my head and push past but she moved closer. 'You need some help,' she said.

I looked at her straight, for the first time. She was in her twenties, maybe, quite short, built like a PE teacher, in a padded ethnic sort of jacket. She had cropped hair and a well-scrubbed look. 'I'm OK . . . ' I said.

'No, you're not.' She tossed a glance back at the grim hotel. 'I'm going to take you for a coffee,' she said. 'If you don't like what you hear, you can go. You have another plan?'

'Laura-Lee,' she said. 'With a hyphen. I'm from the Safe House. It's a place for young people in housing need.'

'A social worker?' I said. 'No, thanks . . . '

'Don't worry,' she said. 'You don't have to tell me your name, or where you come from. We're a charity. We just don't want to see kids like you out on the streets at night.' What did she mean: *kids like me?* She was to the point, OK—bright-eyed, straight-talking, maybe a bit too straight. She was talking like she knew me, when she didn't. Just then the waitress came up, with a trolley of cakes and pastries. 'Choose,' said Laura-Lee, and if I'd been meaning to speak I didn't, because my mouth was flooding with saliva. It was days on end since I'd had something really sweet.

'And no,' she said, 'I'm not a social worker. I've been where you are. I know what it looks like out of that window.' As if on cue, the café window blurred and spattered with a shower of rain.

'This *Safe House* . . . ' I said, wiping my lips. 'What is it? Something religious?' I said. That would explain that slightly too-bright look about her eyes. She'd be some happy-clappy sort of Christian.

'No,' she said. 'We just don't like to see people screwing up their lives. Not when they've got so much potential.' She licked the flakes of apple strudel off her fingers, one by one, then gave me a straight look and smiled. 'Young man like you, in a place like Henderson's Hotel? That's not what you want.'

'What do I want, then?' I tried to make it sound a bit feisty, but by now I was pretending. The coffee was frothy, hot and sharp and very good, and I kind of liked this woman. She was still looking at me, almost teasing, and when our eyes met we both smiled.

'Who knows?' she said. 'You tell me, when you've had a deep bath and a good night's sleep. Would you rather go home?' She laid a hand on her shoulder bag as if she'd have reached in, if I'd said Yes, and given me the fare.

A pause. I shook my head. 'Well, then,' she said. 'What have you got to lose?' She looked at me straight, as if it was a real question and it had an answer. What *did* I have to lose? There was an answer, of course, but I wouldn't find out what it was for some time yet.

The Safe House was a shop front, in the cheaper end of town. Next door on one side was a launderette, on the other a sign said To Let and looked as if it had been saying it for some time. There were charity shops—the same junk laid out in a whole variety of causes. The Safe House wasn't a shop, though, and the windows had their blinds drawn. 'The office,' said Laura-Lee leading me through to a side door. She unlocked it and I followed her up the steep dark stairs.

The room was small, with just a bed, a wardrobe, and a window. After Henderson's, it felt like five-star. 'Where are your things?' said Laura-Lee, and I told her about the bag I'd lost back at the squat. 'Forget that. We give a small grant, to get people started. I'll come down the shops with you.' When we got back, I had one spare of everything and an overnight kit.

'All this . . . it's on the house?' I said, at the door of my room.

'On the Safe House,' she smiled. 'Make yourself at home. There'll be a couple of others back later. You can meet up over supper. Now, you need to catch up on some sleep.'

It was true. 'By the way,' she said, looking back from the stairs, 'you can go on with the human statue business. You've got a gift for it.'

'Pardon? How . . . ?' But I was slow and sleepy. She was out of sight already, and I was yawning. It could wait until this evening, but I did want to ask her, 'How did you know about that?'

I went out like a light. I hadn't slept well for a week and yesterday had been the last straw. Everything had started feeling like a dream. I might get a kick from my dreams but I like to be able to wake up. It was as though I was watching a film of myself out of sync; I felt my lips move and I heard the sound, but they weren't quite in time. I thought of the look in the eyes of some of the beggars I'd seen, and thought: yes, that's how it gets, if you can never really sleep. I thought of my day as a statue, how I'd started to feel as if I was watching it all from somewhere slightly else. You hear about out-of-body experiences, when someone in a car crash or on the operating table finds themselves looking down on their body from above. Hadn't I been part way there, watching myself, the crowd around me, and the grey man watching—all without moving my eyes?

I was back in the alleyway now, and he was watching. Things had been getting dreamlike in real life, but this dream was lucid: I knew I was dreaming and could do what I wanted. I can look from somewhere else, I thought, and with an uncomfortable feeling like turning my brain around inside my skull I brought my attention to bear on the place to my left, where my eyes couldn't see. There was the shadow of the abbey. I could feel the edge of it, a straight edge that went lumpy at intervals where the shadow of a gargoyle jutted out. And one of the gargoyle shadows was the man. Everything in this way of seeing was in shades of night-sight grey, and he was an outline, slightly darker. His face was the darkest part of him, and in the middle of that, two patches of the deepest dark of all: his eyes. I knew if I looked into them for more than a moment, I could fall in, sucked into the space behind them, which was as icy and airless and beyond all hope as Pluto.

He was talking, quietly, steadily, maybe not to me. It was like the first words he'd said in the street, before I could make out the accent, so it could have been another language or a code I had to crack. The voice was level, rasping slightly, with no pause for breath. It could have been made by a machine that pumps air through the larynx of a man, and as the chill of that thought struck me I startled awake, because there was another voice alongside his voice, equally hurried and urgent and a bit too soft to hear.

A woman's voice. Laura-Lee's. I was awake now, on

this new bed with its clean crisp sheets. The angle of light from the window had shifted. I was stiff. I must have slept for hours.

I blinked and sat up, trying to shake the last of the dream out of my head, but the voices went on, first one then the other, rather softer in the waking world than in my sleep. They were there, as close as if the two of them were talking just outside my door. I was crouched on the bed now; my skin was prickling. No, they weren't outside the door. Through a wall? I crept up close and listened— no, they were behind me, in the air. Then I looked at the window and yes, there was a small plastic ventilator in the pane. As I pressed my face up close to it, I could hear the voices clearer, coming up from a window, I guessed, in the room below.

First it had been curiosity, then a kind of thrill of strangeness, but now it was fear. She knew him. Him, the grey watcher . . . He was in the Safe House, now. They were talking seriously, talking business. Bit by bit, the thoughts jigsawed together. Laura-Lee had known about the statue business. Had she watched me . . . or had *he*? She had been waiting for me outside Henderson's Hotel. How did she know? Had he followed me? Had he, or she, or someone else I didn't know about, been watching all the time?

I was wide awake now, and forcing my shoes on. There'd been a moment yesterday when I'd gone looking for him, this grey watcher, but that dream knew better. My first reaction, in the alley, had been right. Run, run away from that terrible dark coldness in those eyes. Calmly, I told myself, calmly and no panic, that's what I was going to do now. Run. I was getting out of here.

8

I was out on the landing, treading lightly, with my overnight bag in my hand. I'd rammed everything in, spare clothes, the Mozart stuff and all. I wasn't going to be caught out again. I eased the door shut carefully, so that it wouldn't bang. There was a spring on it, and for the last centimetre it stuck. The moment I took my hand off it, it sprang shut with a little thud. I froze.

Downstairs, there was the rise and fall of Laura-Lee's voice, then the grey man's, flat and low. After a minute, I breathed again and started to tiptoe downstairs. I was trying to remember the layout of the place. If they were in the shop front, I was stuck. But it didn't sound like that. Hadn't there been a little room off at the back? That was where they must be. Unless the door was open, and it didn't sound as though it was, I should have five steps, a couple of seconds, to the front door and away.

But I mustn't waste time thinking. When you're trying to creep down stairs quietly, they creak—any child knows that. Just move. They were talking now, but they might finish any moment.

Relax, I told myself. Just walk, like any normal person, any normal afternoon. Even if they heard me, well, what could they do? I was going for a walk, that's all. It's a free country, isn't it? At the foot of the stairs, there was the door that Laura-Lee had unlocked. I felt for the catch, that should have been on the inside of the Yale lock, and it wasn't there. No handle, nothing. I got my fingers in the crack at the side and tried to pull; it didn't budge. Locked. I was trapped.

The voices had stopped. Had they heard me? I backed up the staircase, wincing at each step. I listened on the landing for the click of a door. It didn't come, not yet.

They'd locked me in. A trap. My heart was thudding, only one thought in my head: *Get out of here*. I ran back to my bedroom. Think, fast . . . I bunched up the bedclothes, with the pillow in them. Now . . .

Outside the window, there were shed roofs, tatty gardens . . . all further down than I'd expected. The place was built on a hillside; what was the first floor from the front was the third at the back. At any other time, you might have said it was a lovely view.

The sash window was stuck, or maybe they'd screwed the bottom half in place; it didn't move, but the top half gave a little. Once it was open a crack, I hung my whole weight on it, and it jerked down, inch by inch. When it jammed, there was a gap that I could just about imagine squeezing through. I stuck my head out, and saw two things that made all the difference in the world. At the back of the next house was an iron fire escape. And there was a ledge. A step down from the sill, it was no more than a foot's width, but if I could edge along it . . . ? It was a crazy idea, and maybe I'd have thought better of it, except just then I heard the grey man's voice, much clearer now, begin to laugh. I've never heard a laugh that sounded less amusing. Ack-ack, it went, and went on, as sharp as a cough.

I could get myself out. It was holding my things that was the problem. By the time I'd scrambled one arm and my left leg up and over, I suddenly wished I'd packed two carriers, not one bulging canvas bag. As I slithered my weight through the gap, the top pane creaked as if it might just shatter, then I made contact with the outer windowsill.

And the bag stuck. I tugged. I tugged harder, and harder, then the handle snapped and it fell back inside. For a moment I considered climbing back in to get it, then the laughter stopped abruptly, and the silence after it was worse.

They might be coming upstairs, now. Or they might come out in the back yard, look up and see me. I looked down, and knew that I shouldn't have. For a moment I grabbed at the window frame, as the gardens underneath me seemed to sway. I closed my eyes and took a deep breath: *one . . . two . . . three . . .*

Thank God it was an old house; there were cracks between the stones, where crumbling mortar leaked out. If I could edge my feet along, one step at a time, then two . . . If I could just remember Don't Look Down . . . If, if . . .

I was out of reach now of the window. If they looked out, they wouldn't see. Maybe they'd think I'd fallen. And I could see the corner of the fire escape, not far. There was just the one window to pass on the way, and . . .

One window. I would have to climb past someone's room.

But the whole place was so quiet. There was no one here, except the grey man and Laura-Lee. All of this, the whole place, all that effort, was a trap devised for me.

For the first time since I'd run away, I felt a bit important. And for the first time in my life I thought I'd rather not be. Whatever they were after, those two in there, I wished that the person who'd got it wasn't me. These thoughts were babbling in my head, the way they do when you're trying to blank out one big thing: you're scared, you're scared, you're going to slip and break your back, you'll be in a wheelchair, and they'll get you, and you're scared, you're blind shit scared.

Then I was at the windowsill. One more move, and I

could lean both elbows on it. My face pressed against the cool glass, and for a moment I just sighed and closed my eyes.

When I opened them, I saw a picture like a video on freeze-frame, not quite holding, as the figure on the bed looked up, and saw me, and jumped to her feet. The face came up and the mouth opened, just stopping short of a scream, as she recognized me. It was Swan.

What . . . ? she mouthed, and some kind of swearword. *Help me,* I mouthed at her. *I'm going to fall.*

She was quick when she wanted to be, I'll give her that. Quick thinking, too. Her window didn't slide up, any more than mine, but she got something small, a tea spoon, underneath the beading and prised. It came off with a rip, and the bottom pane swung inwards. I crumpled in with it, and slid onto the floor.

'Jesus!' she said after a moment. 'What . . . ?'

'We've got to get out of here!' The words hardly got out, I was so breathless. Her eyebrows moved together in a frown. 'It's a trap,' I said. 'They've got us locked in!'

'Locked in? You mean the stair door? They've had some break-ins, that's all. They lock it so people can't just walk in off the street. You want to go out, give them a call.'

Them. So she knew about the grey man. Her clear grey eyes had small frown-lines between them as she looked at me.

'You think I'm cracked, don't you?' I said.

'You do a good imitation.'

'You know that *he's* in the building, don't you?' I tried to sound calm, not like the crazy person I was beginning to sound like. 'Him. The one in grey. The creep who watched you . . . '

'His name is Antonin. Yes, it's exciting, isn't it?'

You know when you sit in the bath, a nice big deep one, and can't be fussed to get out, so in the end you hook the plug out with your toe. For a moment nothing seems to happen, then it's as if gravity is getting stronger. Everything that held you up is gurgling away around you, and you're getting heavier, till you can hardly move at all . . . Five minutes ago I'd been fired up, all adrenalin, fight or flight. It was trickling away. I was struggling. 'But . . . he's weird. You've seen his eyes?' I said.

'You bet,' she said. 'Don't they take your breath away? You can tell he's a genius.'

'Genius?' I said. 'I thought . . . I mean, the way he was watching you . . . and me. I thought he was some kind of pervert. I nearly called the police.' But Swan was laughing now. That small accusing frown was gone; for a moment she threw her head back and was laughing. When she looked at me again, there was a pink flush in her cheeks. You could almost call it pretty.

'Call the police?' she said. 'He'd probably have been flattered if you did. He was a big radical, you know, back then.'

'Back when?' I said dumbly.

'You don't know who he is, do you? Antonin Asch, the great actor and director . . . '

'I've never heard of him,' I said.

'Street theatre,' she said. 'Mime, that kind of thing. He was really big in Paris in the Sixties. I don't know much about it; Laura-Lee'll tell you . . . ' She looked at me. 'God, you were really scared, weren't you?'

'I . . . I suppose I was,' I said. She was shaking her head, slowly, but her eyes were kind. I had to trust someone some time; why not her? 'One moment I think one thing, and the next . . . '

'You could have broken your neck out there.' It might have been my wishful thinking, but I think she was saying that she'd have been really sorry if I had. 'Come on,' she

65

said, 'you'd better help me fix this window, seeing as how I busted it for you.'

'Oh . . . thanks, by the way. Did I say that?' She had her back to me now, stretching up rather gracefully, almost on points, to bash the wood into place.

'There,' she said and grinned, as if we had a little secret—as if, for the first time since I'd left home, I had someone *on my side*.

'He *is* scary, though, isn't he?'

'Of course he is. That's part of it. His power. Anyway,' she said, 'he spotted you.'

'I don't understand. I mean, why me? Why not the Tin Man . . . ?'

'Him? Oh, come on! I know you're new to this game, but . . . '

'But even I can see *he*'s rubbish, yes.' I finished her thought, and she smiled. 'I know one thing, though,' I went on. 'You're good.'

She didn't blush or giggle or act flattered. She looked at me for a moment, that was all. Yes, I thought, she's serious about it. A professional.

'What did Antonin say to you?' she said.

'*You have it*. That's what he said. Twice. *You have it*. What did he mean?'

For a moment that tight look came back to her face. 'Did he? He told me I had *possibility*. Don't you take it for granted, either.'

'Hold on,' I said. 'Possibility of *what*?'

'Oh, come on. You've heard them talking at the drop-in. You know what everyone wants.'

'The big break? Any time I mentioned anything like that, everybody clammed up. Don't look like that. You know you did.'

She shrugged. 'What matters now,' she said, 'is that we've got a chance to prove ourselves. A chance, that's all. If you don't measure up, he'll drop you, just like that.'

'That does sound scary,' I said. 'Aren't you worried?'

'Of course I am.' Suddenly her fists clenched, her knuckles went white. One moment she'd been laughing, like a friend. The next, she was spiky and tense, like a stranger again. 'This is the chance,' she said fiercely. 'The one chance. Blow this, and you're nothing. It won't come again.' There was a long pause. 'If you don't know that, you don't know anything. You're better off leaving. Go on,' she said. 'Back to Mummy and Daddy.'

That wasn't fair. I should have been annoyed, and flared back, but the speed of all this seemed to have taken my breath away, and all I said was, 'Do you think I should?'

She should have said No. Instead, she paused, as if she was really considering. 'Probably,' she said. 'Remember: we aren't on the same side. We're rivals. He said *You have it*. He didn't say that to me.' There was that frown again. 'I don't know about you, but I need this. *Need* it. Do what you like, but if you do anything to get in my way . . .'

There was a knocking on the landing. Laura-Lee was at my door. She called my name.

'You can get out now,' Swan said, 'if you want to. I'll stall her for a minute or two. You can climb out of that window again. I won't tell.' I looked in her eyes, and they were pale and cool and level. That flash of anger had gone. For a moment I was imagining myself on a coach, bound for another town, even going home. And what would I be doing, on that journey? I knew. I'd be wondering: where is she now? what's she doing? and what would have happened, what would we have said or done if, just imagine, I'd stayed?

'Nick?' called Laura-Lee again.

67

'Are you going?' she said.

'No.' And then, very slightly, she smiled.

'OK,' she said, then called out. 'Laura-Lee, Nick's here with me. We'll be down in a minute.' And so it was decided. There were times in the next day when I could have turned and walked out, like she said. But I didn't. When Antonin announced, 'We leave tomorrow,' Swan and I exchanged a look, but nodded.

'Leave? Where to?' I said when he was out of earshot.

'Only the best training academy on this planet,' said Laura-Lee. 'There are people out there who would kill for the chance. You don't know how lucky you are.' It was true. I didn't know anything . . . except that if Swan was in this, I was in it too.

Lunchtime next day, we rolled up at the service station. The white van had been a surprise. Inside, it was something else—not quite as swish as a limo, but comfy, with seats round the sides and a bar. There were no windows. I could see a square of road past Laura-Lee, who was up front, driving. I soon gave up trying to spot the road signs. It would all become clear when we got there.

Antonin sat very upright. Swan and I might as well not have been there, for all he noticed us. He stared at the wall opposite as if he could see right through it, maybe to the place we were going. Where that was, nobody said. If anyone spoke, it was Laura-Lee. There was a third kid there, a dark-skinned Welsh guy, and from the moment he climbed in he couldn't stop chattering. He was up from Cardiff, and he had this great routine; he'd show us; he'd heard of these whole streets of human statues somewhere, maybe Amsterdam, maybe Barcelona, and that's where they'd be taking us, or him, at least; he was going to be big-time, you just wait and see. It was only when Antonin climbed in, very silent, that the boasts dried up and, like Swan and me, the Welsh kid found a spot to stare at. You could say we felt embarrassed, but it was stronger than that. His power, Swan had called it. You just knew that when this man had walked on to a stage, a great hush would have fallen on the audience and they'd have held their breaths and waited, even if they had to wait all night.

The service station, when we pulled in, was an anywhere place, with all the usual brand names and the usual crowds. We used the toilets and got treated to a burger like kids on an outing, with Laura-Lee as mum. Then we headed back to the car park.

'One moment . . . ' Antonin spoke for the first time since we'd left. It wasn't just the accent, that French-but-not-quite; he spoke stiffly, as if his voice box had gone rusty from disuse.

'One moment. Soon we will be in a place without telephone. You wish to make a call to anyone, now is the time. The telephone is round the corner back there.' His eyes moved round us, one by one. I could see now where that dark look came from; I had never seen eyes so sunken in their sockets, and the skin around them was purplish-grey, like a bruise. I looked at the floor before his full gaze reached me. I could call Mum now, or even leave a message on the answerphone. Just to say I was OK, that's all. They'd never trace me. Then I thought of Malcolm's voice, and I thought: *no!*

'Yeah,' the Welsh kid said. 'I'll just give my mate Spike a bell. Tell him to eat his heart out. Yay!' He skipped back out of sight.

'Come,' said Antonin, abruptly, and walked out to the car park. Laura-Lee followed him, ushering Swan and me.

'Wait a mo,' I said. 'What about him?'

No one replied. Laura-Lee herded us on. When we were in the van, the engine revving, and the door thudded shut, Antonin spoke.

'No ties,' he said. 'We must have no ties. That boy was looking back over his shoulder.' The van nudged out on to the slip road, and paused, revving.

'Welcome,' said Antonin, in a sudden high voice. He turned and startlingly held out a hand to shake. In the moment Swan and I glanced at each other—*after you, no, after you*—he froze. The hand in mid air, the head canted sideways, and the halfway grin on his face locked, like a freeze-frame on a film. From inside the stuck grin came a little chuckle, rising inside until he gave the short bark that I'd heard once before, when he said *You will laugh!*

'No ties,' he cried. 'No looking back. You see? Now we *go*!'

9

We were nowhere. You know those way-back family holidays, when you'd sit in the back of the car and watch trees and pylons and motorway verges go by like a kind of silent film, with no plot and no characters, and you'd go dazed with boredom? It's the kind of memory that makes me glad I'm not a kid any more. Well, from the back of the van there wasn't even that for me and Swan to watch. It *was* a bit like being kids again, in the back, with Antonin up in the front with Laura-Lee.

It was a relief, too. Early in the journey, in the back with us, he'd seemed to be in a trance, though thinking back I guessed he'd been watching us, without looking, in that spooky way he had. Since the service station all I'd seen was the back of his head but I couldn't get rid of the feeling that he knew what we were doing, somehow, even now.

We didn't talk, Swan and I. We didn't look at each other. Once, Laura-Lee spoke over her shoulder: 'You'll be thirsty. There's juice in the bar,' and Swan and I opened it to find small cartons of orange. It tasted like plastic but we were thirsty, and said thanks, and drank. Every now and then I'd sneak a glance at Antonin, and sometimes I'd peep at Swan, and catch her looking at Antonin too. He didn't move or speak. We hurtled on.

We were on a straight stretch of motorway now and the noise was oddly soothing. Here I was, putting the miles between me and all my life so far—I'd left home,

71

I'd been in a squat, I'd been next best thing to homeless—and I was getting these flashbacks of feeling really small. When I was a baby, Mum used to say, the only way she could get me to sleep was by doing the hoovering or putting the washing machine on. White noise, they call it. White noise in a white van. Everything felt peaceful, calm and slow, and outside the miles must be falling away. I imagined them like one of those flicker-books I got from the shop in the science museum years ago: you flick the corners of the pages and a picture seems to move. 'That's the movies for you,' Dad said. 'A con trick, just an optical illusion . . .'

White van, white noise. White . . . I took another peep, and there was Swan's face, with her eyes closed, still and white. At rest, without the ballerina make-up or the streetwise look, it was a classic profile, slightly Greek, maybe. I could imagine tracing the lines of it with a finger, cool like marble, and the thought sent a little warm shiver through me. Then, as I was looking, her head rolled to one side and she opened her eyes. It might have been because we were both in a daze, but we were looking at each other, straight on, and we didn't look away, the way you're meant to.

'Are you OK?' I said after a moment. Her face screwed up a little, and mouthed something I couldn't make out. With a glance at the back of Antonin's head, I shuffled closer.

'Carsick,' she said faintly. 'I get carsick.'

'Let's ask them to stop.'

'No!' She shook her head—too hard, because she closed her eyes and swallowed. But I got the message. Remember the Welsh boy, his boasting and chattering. Anything might be a test. He'd failed, and we'd dumped him. If we put a foot wrong from now on, where would we be?

'Do you know where we're going?' I whispered. She shook her head. 'Aren't you worried?'

She glanced up, with a wan smile: 'Of course. Aren't you?'

I nodded. Now we'd both admitted it. We might be rivals, like she'd said, but it seemed easier, here, to trust each other. It was like talking with the lights out after dark. I thought how sometimes you get talking to a stranger on a train, and tell each other all kinds of things, because you know in a moment you'll get off and never meet again. No, I thought, no: Swan wasn't going to be a stranger, not from now on. I leaned closer. 'It'll be OK,' I said. 'Whatever happens, let's stick by each other.'

I think she wanted to nod, but as her head went down her eyes closed. For a while she balanced upright, then we went into a bend and she gradually slumped towards me. I felt the warmth of her beside me, the weight of her head on my shoulder, and I could hear her breathing. Asleep, she felt smaller and younger, and I would have put an arm around her, except that I might wake her up and she might move away. I didn't want that to happen.

So there we were: in a locked van, headed for an unnamed somewhere, the big break, the statue academy, fame and fortune . . . if you believed Antonin and Laura-Lee. And who were they? Two people I'd seen for the first time the day before yesterday. All I really knew was that one of them was the most unsettling man I'd ever met. It was mad. And yet, right now, I felt sort of peaceful, with the rise and fall of Swan's slight breathing on my neck.

There was a jolt. Time had passed. The van was going slower, taking bends. Swan stirred and groaned and moved away. Outside the windscreen the sunlight was lower, flickering through the trees. Swan was looking around, as vague as I was. We'd been in suspended animation, both of us. I had no idea where we were.

Antonin was dozing; every now and then he gave a little tremor, like a dog in its sleep. As I watched, we hit a bump, a hump-backed bridge maybe; he gave a small *Hah!* Then he was laughing, soft and rather high. 'The first lesson,' he said, over his shoulder. 'We are not in motion.' He gave that cough-like laugh of his. 'We leave the ground and stay still, relative to the heavenly bodies. The earth rotates beneath us, that is all.'

The van slowed, swung round a corner, and came to a stop, the engine idling. Through the windscreen I could see the metal bars of a gate. They slid open, unasked. 'And now, you see,' said Antonin, 'you think we are still. No! The earth turns at a thousand eight hundred *kilometre* per second. That is how fast he goes, the *immobiliste*, when he is perfectly still. More than the speed of sound. Bang!' The van crunched on gravel and came to a halt. 'The sonic boom . . . It is a wonder you can hear me at all.' Antonin had turned in his seat. Deep in their sockets, his eyes held us, glittering. Were we meant to laugh? Then Laura-Lee had got out and came round to his door. She slid it open and helped him out into the evening air.

'Well?' I turned to Swan. 'What about that? Is that man nuts, or what?'

'He's . . . original,' she said. 'What he said just now . . . it *was* kind of brilliant, wasn't it? I mean, as well as strange.'

'Hmm,' I said.

So this was the academy. We were in a courtyard, with high stone buildings with tangles of ivy, and there were people waiting—a cluster of young people who had to be students, in sweaters and jeans, looking curiously at the van. When Laura-Lee got out there was a quick exchange of hugs. Antonin walked past them all without speaking,

74

though they turned to look at him. 'Come on,' said Laura-Lee, sliding the back door open. The other students clustered round behind her. 'Leave your bags,' she said. 'The guys will take them up.' I must have hesitated, because she laughed. 'Come on, you won't get waited on like this every day! Follow me.'

I glanced at Swan. She was trying to laugh but she looked pale, and it wasn't just feeling carsick. What was this place? Who were these people, laughing as if we were all the best of friends? She looked as lost as I felt. As Laura-Lee turned and led on, I reached out a hand and touched Swan's shoulder. It was the kind of movement that a person can ignore, or seem to—so light that it could have been an accident. I rather expected that she'd move away, after Laura-Lee, but no. She didn't turn to look at me; her hand came up and for a second, a long second that felt like several minutes, she let it rest on top of mine, and I didn't move mine away.

The house was an old one, maybe grand, and this was the back entrance—the stable yard, I guessed, in the days of horses. Laura-Lee led us up stairs and into a high room with sofas and armchairs scattered round, and a couple of big saggy beanbags. It was tatty and friendly and nothing that matched anything else, like all the student bedsits in town thrown into one. 'This is the Cool Room,' she said. 'Where we come to cool down, chill out. You're going to need it sometimes.' She threw herself down in a sag bag. Swan and I sat on a sofa, cautiously. 'Look, here are some of the gang now,' said Laura-Lee, as two or three of them walked in. 'Swan . . . Nick . . . '

The three flopped down around us. 'Hi,' said the wild-haired guy who was struggling to grow himself a bushy moustache. 'New kids on the block! I'm Albie.' He gave the face-fur an apologetic tug. 'I'm working on Einstein,' he said.

75

'Hi!' chirped one of the girls. She had blue wide eyes and was small, neat, pretty, with that look some girls with little faces have, as if each feature is outlined in ink. 'I'm Ange. I do angels.' She turned to the girl next to her, whose smile lit up on cue. 'And you're going to love it here. Isn't she, Maisie?'

'Yeah.' The other spoke softly, in a mid-Atlantic drawl. She might have been there for the contrast with Ange: everything about her looked sort of healthy and country-ish, like an advert for a new thing that nearly tastes like butter, though as she leaned forwards there was something a bit too intense in her eyes. I wondered if Antonin gave them lessons in The Look. 'Guess all this looks kind of new. Don't worry. You'll be just fine. Won't they?' And the three of them nodded together. That's when I twigged: they hadn't just happened to walk in. This was a welcoming party. They'd done this routine before.

'You'd think it was a holiday,' said Laura-Lee, 'to listen to these guys. But you're going to work hard too.'

'You'll want to,' Ange put in. 'It's a privilege . . . '

'You've been selected,' Laura-Lee went on, 'because Antonin thinks you have potential. You've convinced him—so far—that you're serious.' I looked at her. She dropped the banter suddenly, and her voice was serious. 'The training you'll get here is the best in the world. We don't do drink or drugs or smoking. We don't fool around. We're here to keep each other on-task, understand? Good, and if you can take it, you'll be the elite.'

In the pause that followed, none of the others stopped smiling, but their eyes were watching us. What were we meant to say?

'We'll get to work abroad, is that right?' I said. 'Someone mentioned Amsterdam and Barcelona.' It seemed right to sound keen.

'We don't think about that,' said Maisie. 'I mean, sure, we all want to be rich and famous and stuff, but it's about more than that, isn't it? I mean, it's about *doing* it. It's a way of life.'

Swan looked at Laura-Lee. 'When do we get to study with Antonin?' she said. From Laura-Lee's face, that seemed to be the right question, unlike mine.

'When the time's right. Don't worry. He'll be watching you.' Laura-Lee stood up. 'You must be tired,' she said. 'I'll show you where you bed down. And the kitchen. You need to eat.'

'Can I show them the grounds?' said Maisie.

Laura-Lee looked at us. 'If they want to. Take a look. Your bags will be up in the guys' room,' she said to me, and to Swan, 'And yours in the women's.'

'The guys' room?' I said, after Laura-Lee had gone. 'You mean, like a dormitory?' Even in the *squat* I'd had my own room.

'Sure!' said Maisie. 'We're all in this together. It's not a hotel, you know. It's a community. You'll just love the people. Come with me. I want to show you *everything*. You won't believe your eyes!'

There was a passageway so dark it could have been a tunnel, with flagstones worn by years of feet. Then just as our eyes got accustomed there were steps and we followed Maisie up into a dazzle of light. The sun had shifted right in front of us, and I shielded my eyes. We'd come under the house and emerged on a terrace, and here was everything the lord and lady of this place must have owned. The lawns sloped down, to a glint of a lake, a fringe of reeds and weeping trees. In a little bay, a quaint low boathouse stood with one end knee-deep in the water. Further round there was a little peninsula dark with

77

rhododendron bushes. Beyond, the woods rose steep and thick, closing out the world outside. It was perfect, and perfectly private, like a whole small kingdom.

'What *is* this place?' I said under my breath. 'Where are we?'

Maisie turned with a smile. 'We just call it the Place,' she said. 'Kind of Paradise, isn't it? Even if it has seen better days.' She was right. The whitewash was peeling round the edges of the wide bay window. Still, I thought of the College back home, where I'd planned on going, with its glass and concrete blocks out by the ring road. I couldn't complain.

'Oh, and there's the Folly.' Among the rhododendrons there were a few white columns placed just so, to reflect in the lake.

'It's like a stage set,' I said.

'Yeah,' said Maisie. '*Life is theatre. Theatre is life*. That's what *Antonin* says.' That slight stress on the name: I recognized it. In Young Stagers there were girls who just had to remind you they were friends with the oldest kids there, the ones who were nearly professional, and the teachers too. They would keep on mentioning a name, a first name, like that. 'Meant to be a kind of Greek temple,' she went on. She'd done this guided tour before. 'But they built it half fallen down, if you get what I mean. Way back, the Earl or whatever used to pay a guy to sit in it and be a philosopher, dressed up like an ancient Greek. I guess he had to watch for when someone was coming and start thinking. Bit like an Immo, really.'

'Immo?' I said. Somehow it was always me who asked the obvious questions; Swan just looked and listened, and it was me who would look stupid. Swan was definitely not stupid. She had the knack of putting on a look as if, whatever I'd just asked, she knew already. Maisie hesitated, head on one side.

78

'Course,' she said, 'you're new. Immobilist.' That word again, the one Antonin used in the van. 'Don't worry, you'll pick it up. We're like one big family here, you know.'

Round the corner of the house, the windows were suddenly high. Exotic plants—date palms, huge cacti, creepers with bell-shaped scarlet flowers—pressed up against the panes. 'The Orangery,' said Maisie. I peered in through glass gone half opaque with dust. There was a row of stone plinths, some with statues, some not . . . and one empty wicker chair. On the floor by the chair was a wine glass with a slender stem. So . . . not abandoned. Someone went there to be alone—not one of the students, I guessed. Maybe Antonin?

'What a place!' I said. 'He must be loaded, Antonin.'

Maisie stopped. 'It's not *Antonin's*,' she said, slightly indignant. 'He doesn't *own* things. None of us do. Like I said, we're a *community*.'

'Still,' I said, 'it must be someone's.'

Maisie looked at me, not certain now. 'Well, Dom, of course. Don't worry,' she said brightly. 'You'll pick things up as you go along.'

Dom? Who, or what? I didn't ask. Among the hundreds of things she'd told us on our guided tour there were a few she hadn't mentioned—basic things, like where we actually *were*. But why deny it, this place *was* a kind of Paradise. Maisie seemed happy in it, and she was no cleverer than Swan or me. There was money around, too: you could almost smell it. Wherever we were, it was a million miles from Henderson's Hotel, and whatever we needed to know, we'd find out when the time was right.

Maisie led us down stone steps and we were in the formal gardens. Formal, but with just a touch of wilderness. The grass was edged and trimmed, but creepers hung straggling from each wall. We went through an arch, a

79

rusty gateway, down decaying steps. On the next narrow terrace a bed of roses surprised us, just before we saw it, with a wave of scent. It was almost too much. Lower still, there were thickets of bamboo so dense I half expected pandas in them, and when a bird screeched overhead I looked up for a scarlet macaw or toucan, though it was only a jay. Everything was lush, with a moist heat, a tropical feel, in the air. Through a low arch, and there was a whispery sound, like rushing water, and we stood in the silvery light of a glade of eucalyptus trees.

The lowest of the gardens was most formal of all. There was a circular pond with a fountain dribbling from a huge conch shell hoisted on some Greek god's back. There was a stone nymph in a grotto. Everywhere there was a heavy dose of Greek and Roman, like the kind of stately gardens Mum and Dad used to drag me round when he was still at home. I was too young to see the attraction then, and I had to walk slowly and not scuff the gravel paths. After they'd separated, Mum used to say it was typical: he was so tight-arsed, obsessional, that was why he had a thing about gardens like that. Maybe that's why it had a gloomy sort of taste for me, those neat little squares and semi-circles, and the tidy beds of tiny roses, and the sad-faced statues on their plinths.

Maisie swept out an arm theatrically. 'The Sculpture Garden. Bet you can't tell which of them are real.'

I looked round. There were statues everywhere. Some of them couldn't be human: there was a deer with antlers, and a wild boar; there were god-like figures more than life size, or figures not carved whole but sculpted in a kind of frieze. And the god with the conch surely couldn't be . . . or could he? That nymph in the grotto, now I looked at her . . . ?

And the copy of the Venus De Milo, with the famous arms snapped off below the shoulders. No, I thought. *No*. I don't normally imagine things as sick as that. It was something about this place; it was wonderful . . . and all a bit too much.

Above the walls and creepers, the topmost storey of the house was in sight, almost leaning over us. The turrety windows looked blank and yet . . . why did I feel someone was in there, watching? Yes, it was Paradise, but in Antonin's world—or was it Dom's world?—someone *would* be watching. What did I expect?

10

One thing you learn never to do in prison, so I've heard, is ask the other prisoners what they're in for. Telling them what you've done is as bad, if not worse. That always struck me as strange. I mean, if you've been brought up in a comfortable family you expect the occasional lecture on the right way to behave. When my grandma was around she used to call it *etiquette*. You don't expect convicts to have it, even murderers and people in for GBH. Then you realize they have to; if they didn't, there'd be riots every day.

This was nothing like prison. Looking round the dining room that evening, it looked better than a canteen, more like a slightly faded grand hotel. There was even a chandelier in the middle of the ceiling, though the food was pushed out of a battered steel hatch. There was a cork board with a cooking rota pinned up and I got a whiff of how things were going to work, or not work, in this place. 'How come I'm always on washing up after Albie,' someone was grumbling, 'and how come he always burns the macaroni cheese?' That at least was like home. But after the welcoming party, no one really spoke to me.

Maisie had taken us up to the rooms. My heart sank at the sight of the men's—it might have been a long gallery in its heyday, with those tall windows looking out across the view, but now it was halfway between a crash-pad and a dormitory. At least we didn't have bunks, and the twenty-odd beds were pushed into alcoves and corners at all angles, but the whole place had a slightly sweaty, slightly antiseptic, institution smell.

No one was up in the room, so I unpacked my bag into my small locker. If I'd brought anything with me—those dog-eared posters, postcards from friends on their holidays, all the stuff from my old bedroom—I'd have been blu-tacking it to the wall, making the little alcove round my bedhead feel a bit like home. Then I noticed that nobody else had done it either. Several beds had just a photograph or two pinned up. Not Mum or Dad, not girlfriends—*No ties!* Antonin had said—but what I knew must be themselves in costume, in their human statue pose. The first thing they'd see when they woke up in the morning, and the last thing at night . . . *You're here to work.* Laura-Lee had said it with a smile, but she'd meant it. *This is not a holiday.*

A few beds had another picture, black and white and fading. When I looked close at one I saw a street scene, with a foreign feel about it, and old-fashioned cars. In the middle of the pavement and drawing a crowd there was a human statue, very tall and thin. He had almost no costume; instead, with some cunning body-painting he'd darkened the spaces between his naked ribs, and whitened them so they stood out like bare bone. His head was shaved and the pits of his eyes were black; he'd drawn his lips back till they vanished. The grin of a skull. This human statue was a living skeleton. And, do I need to tell you, it was Antonin.

There was a hollow gonging sound somewhere. The door clicked and Laura-Lee looked in. 'Supper! Get a move on.' In the dining room, she sat me down beside her, near the end of one long table. Swan wasn't down yet. A couple of the others looked up but this time she didn't introduce me, and they got on with their eating. Antonin wasn't there. Maisie, so talkative earlier, had become polite,

83

passing the water or the sauce, but that was all. Every now and then I opened my mouth to ask a question, but something told me No, that isn't what you do. The etiquette. Just *explain*, I thought. But no one was going to, not yet.

There were questions everywhere—behind the bushes in the gardens, behind the faded furniture that lined the once-grand rooms—if only I knew what they were. Then again, if I knew what the questions were, I wouldn't need to ask. I'd be an insider, like Maisie and the others. *You'll soon pick it up*, she'd said. But I was starting to get the drift: ask a question at the wrong time and you might just fail some kind of test. I couldn't even ask Swan. I'd hoped we'd sit together, but when she appeared she nodded at me, that was all, quite quick and stiff, and went to sit two tables away. I tried to catch her eye, but she'd sat with her back to me, and I felt a sudden twinge as I thought of the back of the van, of her head on my shoulder, and the moment in the courtyard when her hand took mine. That was . . . oh, all of an hour ago. And now? I'd see her later. So I thought.

So I ate up Albie's burnt macaroni, and if I was on washing up no one had told me, so waited for the next thing to happen. And it didn't. After they'd eaten, people drifted away, and when I came back from taking my plate to the hatch Swan was gone. I ran up the stairs, but there was no sign of her. I didn't even know which way the women's room was. A couple of the guys gave me a funny look as I stood on the landing, lost, but nobody spoke. I wandered down to the dining room; it was empty, except for the clatter of washing up in the kitchen out the back. I found a couple of big rooms with nobody in them, though one had a huge dance-mirror on one wall. The young man who stared back at me from it looked as lost as I felt, and pale with tiredness. I found my way back to the Cool

84

Room, and there was the sound of a TV in there, but on the threshold I stopped. As I stood in the doorway no one turned; they went on lounging round and chatting, in their tight small groups. Another time I might have plonked myself down and said *Hi!* But I was yawning. I'd come so far today—how far, I didn't know, but it felt like jet lag. I stood there a moment. No one looked up. So I went to bed.

Bang. Where was I? In the dark. Not home, not the squat. There were windows in all the wrong places. There were people moving: huge dark figures rearing round me, and the smell of burning. I'd been deep asleep, how long I couldn't guess. I'd gone up to the dormitory at the end of supper, feeling dog-tired, still groggy from the van. I must have fallen straight to sleep, so this must be one of my dreams.

I blinked, and the nightmare figures should have faded but they didn't. They were real—not as huge as they'd seemed, because the rearing figures were their shadows on the walls behind them, shuddering to and fro with the flame. I looked at the faces of the real shapes around me, and they were flat, mask-like, with holes for eyes. Then there was nothing but dazzle as someone thrust a burning stick in front of my eyes. I threw up my hands but someone yanked at the sheets, which rolled me over and I hit the ground, hard, with my shoulder. There were hands all round me, dragging at the T-shirt and boxer shorts I was wearing, pushing and pulling till I sprawled over, naked; then there were several of them leaning on me, crushing the breath from my chest as they yanked my hands behind me, tightening a knot that bit into the flesh, and hurt. As I gasped, something plasticky tight was slapped across my mouth, wound round two, three times,

85

as I thrashed and struggled. I knew the stories, how they wrap kitchen clingfilm round your face—it doesn't leave a mark—and you're dead within minutes, kaput.

I was on my feet now. The hands had grabbed me by the armpits, hauling me upright, and my legs nearly crumpled. Keep calm. I could breathe, as long as I didn't start panicking. Calm . . . But the one with the fire was dancing, jabbing it towards me every time I opened my eyes, so I flinched and staggered. 'Keep still!' Someone pushed me forward, and I closed my eyes and swayed. 'Still!' another voice echoed. Then everything stopped. I opened my eyes to see they'd stepped back, in a circle round me. There was a low breath—*hahh!*—from the ring of masks.

Behind them, I could see, the beds were empty. No point in shouting, even if I could have. These were my room mates. There was no one else to hear.

For a moment they were still, then they were circling round me, an inner and an outer ring circling opposite ways until my head began to spin—flat faces in the firelight and shadowy bodies they didn't quite fit. They were in costume, dressed for statuing maybe, but wearing each other's faces, and the circling got faster, and then with a rush they'd grabbed me. Somebody jerked a blindfold on me from behind, then they were dragging me out, half pushing, half lifting me as I slipped and stumbled on the stairs.

The night air hit me. I was naked. I felt gravel underfoot, then they pulled me and I stumbled, grazing my knee. They hauled me upright. I felt damp grass as they dragged me downhill, almost at a run. I could hear their breathing like dogs on the scent, and I stayed limp. There were other sounds—wind in the trees, getting closer, and in a minute we were pushing through undergrowth, sharp twigs and nettles. Then there was another sound.

86

Water, running. Not trickling, but rushing with a steady tearing noise that made me think of the river back home, behind the factories where it goes suddenly still, to the edge of the V-shaped weir.

We stopped. It was loud now, as they spun me round a few times, till everything swirled. Then one of them pulled off the blindfold. I staggered for a moment, looking into a drop.

I was right on the edge . . . the edge of what I couldn't make out, not at first, but it went down a long way. Down in the darkness, lit by patchy moonlight, was a steady rush of foam. It was white water, funnelling in and downwards through a concrete culvert, getting faster, till . . . Just where it vanished underground, the water rucked up, bits of branches and rubbish tangling round the sharp teeth of a metal grille.

'Keep still!' It was a sharp hiss just behind me and as I turned the voices echoed, always out of sight: 'Still! Still!'

I could have lost my footing then, but they caught me by the arms. For a moment I thought they were going to heave me over, but they held me balanced there. The sweat of fear was drying on my skin and I was shuddering. Some of the others had ducked out of sight; then they were back, heaving something between them, and I saw with a cold shock what they had in mind for me. It was a plank, and they were heaving it out to bridge the culvert. That's what I thought, then with another shudder saw what they meant. No, it wasn't a bridge—just a plank out into mid-air. One of them jerked the blindfold on again.

'What's your name?' It was the voice behind me.

'Nick . . . '

'No!' Somebody slapped me, hard, on the cheek. 'You are a statue. What's your name?'

'M-Mozart?'

'Amadeus! Your name is Amadeus.'

'Amadeus,' other voices chimed.

'Good, now show us how still you can be. As if your life depended on it.' There was a whoop of laughter, and they were spinning me around again. The noise of the water was everywhere. Where was the edge? They manhandled me forwards, till I felt cold slimy wood beneath my feet. It gave a little with my weight and theirs as hands behind me pushed me, pushed me further . . . 'Still, Amadeus!' came a whisper, as hands turned me round a few times more, then the plank quivered. They had left me. I was on my own.

Feet. I had to think with my feet. If I thought with my head, the world was swaying, spinning. Think feet. I eased them a little apart and waited till the spinning slowed down. I eased a toe further, then jerked it back. I'd touched the edge of the plank. I mustn't think what was beneath me. But I did think, and the rush of the water seemed to rise all round me, coming from every direction I didn't expect. I teetered. Think with your feet, Amadeus! Think still . . .

I felt for the edge again, this time on purpose. Yes. Thank God I was barefoot. Leaning my weight on one foot, I traced the edge with the toe of the other. But which way was back to the bank? If only they would laugh or jeer now, I'd know where they were. But there was no sound but the water. I knew I was shuddering—from the cold or the strain in my legs, I didn't know. Feet: that was all that mattered. Very slowly, I started easing my weight on to one foot, then the other, centimetres at a time, shuffling, feeling for the edge, and breathing, trying not to think.

Then I touched it: nothing. The end of the plank. With a rush of vertigo I felt the space all round me. No. Don't panic. I knew where I was now. I just had to inch my way back, steadily. Quickly, but steadily. Mustn't notice that my legs were aching with the tension, and the shuddering was getting worse. I was overbreathing, my pulse rattling. If I could have opened my mouth I'd have been gulping air in, but I couldn't. Sparks of light were flickering behind my blindfold. Then a wave of faintness rushed up through me. I felt myself going, and made one last lurch towards safety, but the wood was slimy and my back foot went. Something hit me—a blow on the shoulder then square in the back, and I was still.

There was a sound of cheering. Even before the thought could form—*I'm not dead*—I could feel them all round me, untying my hands and peeling off the blindfold and the gag. There were torches all round me, lighting up the faces—not masks, human faces—that were smiling, laughing. They were easing me upright, almost gently, and one of them had a blanket to wrap round me.

'Brilliant!' said one. 'You did it.'

And another: 'Hey, Amadeus, you were great!'

I didn't reply. I was staring at the plank, not understanding. Why was I here on the flat grass, slightly winded, and not down in the rushing water, dead? Maybe because the plank hadn't been over the culvert. But I'd seen it. Yes, but then they'd blindfolded me and spun me round some more. They'd moved it. They'd done this before. There was a low bank where they'd wedged it, close enough to the edge to get the sound of water, but I'd never been more than two feet off the ground.

They were holding me now, all the lads from the house, between them, patting me on the back and aching shoulder. 'Good man, Amadeus,' one of them said, close to my ear. 'We've all been through it. But you were brilliant.'

'Party time!' whooped another behind me, and a champagne cork popped past my ear.

'Am-a-deus, A-ma-deus!' someone sang out like a football chant. 'You're in, man. You're one of us now!'

89

11

'One hell of a party,' said a voice. 'You really went for it.'

I was in bed, somehow, but my crumpled clothes and the pain in my head said that the odd stray images in my head were not a dream. There was torchlight, voices singing, and a conga through the forest. There was standing by the lakeside, laughing at the noises ducks make in the dark. There was turning back to face the house up the hillside looking down on us, and thinking: home! And some time later there was lying on my back on the grass, trying to hum *'Eine Kleine Nachtmusik'*, looking up at the moon as it sank and the sky the other way was growing light.

I opened my eyes and there was a face looking down at me. 'Ouch,' I said. 'What happened to the No Drink rule?' I recognized him vaguely from the goings-on last night—a little guy with a sharp pixie-ish face that he could suddenly stretch into a shockingly wide grin. He did it now.

'A special occasion. I'm Hob, by the way. Short for . . . No. let's keep it at Hob.'

'I'm Nick . . . ' I said, from habit.

'No. *Amadeus*. Let's stick to the rules. Nick was then— the big bad world outside. This is now.' He let the grin drop. 'You don't want to go back, do you?'

I lay back and closed my eyes. The pictures in my mind were sorting themselves into shape. There was me walking the plank. The rush of water. The terror. Then they'd been all around me, new friends, saying, 'You're one of us now.' One moment I'd been all fired up, the adrenalin pumping and then . . . relief! I could have flared up—after all, they'd made a fool of me. But no, they were all over me, slapping my back and grinning: *well done, Amadeus, welcome.* And suddenly it had all seemed very funny. Then corks started popping and somebody slipped out a bottle of something almost tasteless that burned on my tongue— and as the fire of it slid down inside me I stopped shivering and looked around to see the others' faces lit up by the same warm glow. Now I knew why no one had welcomed me at supper: they were waiting for the moment. This was the ritual, the initiation. And I'd done all right; I'd passed the test; I was in.

'Well? *Do* you want to go back?' said the face above me. Hob: yes, I could see it. Hob . . . Hobgoblin, that must be his stage name, like it seemed I would be Amadeus. I'd played Puck once—we did *Midsummer Night's Dream* at school—but I'd never looked the part, the way this guy did. Then he grinned his happy-gargoyle grin again, and I saw why they said Hobgob. He was watching me seriously now, as if he was genuinely worried, like a friend. I shook my head—carefully. I had a pain like a spike in my brain.

'Where to?' I said and meant it. 'Anyway, where *are* we?'

'Couldn't tell you,' he said.

'That's another of the rules?'

'No. I mean I *don't know*. It's part of the ethos: total dedication to the art. *No ties.*' He leaned closer and lowered his voice. 'Don't take it too seriously. Just look out for yourself. It's a pretty good deal, considering.' He stood up. 'We don't go out. Got all we need here. The locals aren't particularly friendly—think we're some kind of anarchist commune or something. We keep ourselves to ourselves. Now, shift yourself. Let's get some breakfast.'

91

After two mugs of coffee I began to sit up and take notice. The dining room was full, with everyone clumped round long tables. 'Smells like porridge today,' said Hob. 'I'll get you some.' He vanished into a kitchen sort of place where people were jostling, helping themselves. I looked round. There was Maisie and Ange from yesterday. Where was Swan? Where had she been last night? Had she been there, and seen . . . ? I cringed inside. But there'd been no girls. Clearly, the ritual was a men thing.

Then I saw her, in the furthest corner. She must have felt my stare, because she glanced up and our eyes should have met, except she looked straight down again. No smile, no sign of recognition. Then she was talking to the girl beside her, like the best of friends.

Maisie sat down beside me. 'Hi!' she said, so brightly that I winced. The sound of knives and spoons on plates was hurting me. 'Sorry,' I said. 'Last night . . . '

'Amadeus . . . ' she said slowly, as if trying the name out for taste. 'Yes, I like it.' So she knew.

'Was that just for me?' I said. 'Or does everyone . . . ?' She was nodding. 'Girls too?'

Her look went cool; her lips pursed. I was asking too much. I guessed everyone knew what happened on the first night, but you didn't talk about it. I was one of them now, an insider. Enough said.

Amadeus. There was no Nick here; he'd been left way behind me, in the outside world. No past. *No ties!* That was Antonin's test. Everyone he brought here must have nothing to lose, or something they wanted, desperately, to leave behind.

Hob slid a plate of steaming goo in front of me. 'You a syrup man?' he said and put a saucer-full beside it.

'Thanks,' I said. Inside me, I felt a flush of the warmth from last night, when I'd been naked and shivering and they'd come and wrapped the blanket round me. We were

92

all on the same side. I thought back to the drop-in café, and the Stone Saints and the Tin Man, and the squat. For the first time since I'd left home, I was among friends. The wobbly feelings I'd had yesterday felt like a bad dream; it had been the tiredness, the jet lag sensation, which had left me spooked and slightly paranoid. Now I looked across the room, across heads I still didn't recognize, and all of them seemed a bit like distant cousins, strangers but still family.

One big family: that's what Maisie had said. A *community*. The only person in the room who seemed a hundred miles away was Swan.

First thing each day, without fail, would be an hour of practice. The Work, they called it. Maisie took me in hand. 'Most of the Work,' she was saying, 'is in plain clothes. So we have to really *feel* it, not rely on props. That's what Antonin says.'

'And Antonin watches?'

'Maybe. You never know. When you've worked with him, you get to feel he's always watching, like he's really part of you.' Her eyes had that bright look again, like someone in a fever.

'I think I'll find a private corner, just for now.'

'Don't. We like to practise within sight of each other,' she said. 'That's what we do. And we like to be where Antonin might see us too. Sometimes he stops and has a little session *just with you*.'

'Great,' I said, doing my best to mean it. We followed the others in among the potted palms and plinths that we'd seen through the window. As we walked in, the chat stopped as if we'd walked into church. I looked round, expecting to find Antonin looming like a stern schoolmaster, but there was nobody. The empty wicker chair was still there, empty, with the same wine glass beside it. No one was giving the orders, but people spread out, taking plinths or a free bit of floor, and immediately they were working, without a word being said. I looked round for a place to be. It was weird. In the street, yes, there are people passing. Even when they're ignoring you, you know that you're doing it for *them*. But now? It was like talking to yourself, and that's . . . well, crazy.

Over by the window, right where anyone could see from outside, Swan was into her routine already. Fine, I thought, if she can do it, so can I. I found a space behind a withered prickly pear, and did.

A bell went, and the hour was up. Thank God. My head was throbbing, and the hour had felt like seven. If only I'd been wearing the costume, if I could have tootled my recorder, or just held it . . . No, these people were serious. They worked as if there was somebody standing over them with a whip . . . except there wasn't. Every moment of the hour I'd been watching for Antonin, but he hadn't showed. There was only ourselves, and each other, and a scattering of real statues, really made of stone.

I stepped into the courtyard blinking. As the others streamed out I couldn't help noticing: there was nobody old . . . unless you counted Antonin, and he was sort of ageless. Everyone else looked good—young, fit, in shape. I thought of the Tin Man, working away at it, walking on the spot, always hoping. Someone should tell him. He wouldn't be picked for this, not in a hundred years.

But Antonin . . . ? All the time I'd been practising, the image of him had kept coming back to my mind. Sometimes it was him by the abbey, watching, sometimes the black-and-white photos of him in skeleton kit that people kept above them in their sleep. Weird. The more he didn't show up in the practice session, the more the pictures of him would be there inside my mind. Crossing the courtyard now with Laura-Lee and Maisie, I was trying to bring up the subject. 'He's kind of . . . well, *eccentric*,' I said, 'isn't he?'

'Go on, say it: *mad*.' It was a bloke's voice, just behind me. Its owner, who'd come up beside us, had a mane of curly hair that looked tangled on purpose and a pointy beard.

There was a flash of something sudden, like a warning, in Maisie's eyes. 'We don't use words like *mad*. Antonin says . . .'

The curly guy laughed. He was short, but packed with muscles, the kind you build in the gym. He wore a skin-tight T-shirt to make sure we noticed. 'Mad! He'd take it as a compliment. He'd say you were *ver-r-ry bourgeois* not to say it.' The mimicry was good, and Maisie's expression froze.

'Thank you, Mattheus,' she said primly. 'Antonin's philosophy is very deep. Amadeus knows what I mean.' The guy, Mattheus, gave a shaggy shrug and moved away. Maisie exchanged a silent glance with Laura-Lee, and nodded. 'If I were you,' she said to me, in a low voice, 'I wouldn't have too much to do with him.' She glanced over her shoulder. 'He won't last long.'

'But Antonin . . . ? Is he . . . ?'

'I must show you Antonin's album,' said Maisie. 'Then you'll understand. After the meditation, OK?'

Meditation. That sounded good to me. Maybe I could even snatch a wink of sleep. We were halfway across the courtyard when the sound of the stone saw hit my brain. Through a low dark doorway I glimpsed a racked stand of stone-carver's tools. A broken torso lay propped by the door. Beyond was a shelf of spare parts: some heads, facing this way and that, a foot or two, a clutch of hands.

Beyond that was another door, out into a back yard, where a fug of diesel and stone dust drifted in the sunlight, and I glimpsed a short man built like a small bull in blue overalls.

'One of the groundsmen,' said Maisie. 'He's a stonemason. Some of the statues—the real ones, I mean—are priceless.' I must have raised my eyebrows. 'Dominic's collection is famous, you know. People come from all over the world to buy. We're very lucky to be part of it.' Just then the stonemason's saw bit into something with a teeth-clenching squeal.

'Agh! How can he stand the noise?' I said.

'Deaf,' Maisie said, without smiling. 'Don't try and talk to him. Antonin's the only one he understands.' With that, we ducked through an entrance and into the cool space of the meditation room.

There was Antonin in the centre, waiting as the rest of us filed in and took our places on two lines of hard cushions facing each other, parallel to the walls. He stayed standing, upright, still. He was a heron again, like the first time I'd seen him, in the precinct, watching Swan.

She was in the meditation room already, several places down, so our eyes did not meet. It was strange. I'd tried to bump into her after the practice, but she seemed to slip away. OK. I wasn't going to chase her. Still, I just stepped into the room, and without even looking I knew she was there.

Silence fell without Antonin making a move. 'Good morning, my friends,' he said suddenly, and his face lit up with a slow smile. 'I hope you all slept *ver-r-ry* well.' The smile spread round the room: they all knew. 'We have two new names amongst us. Amadeus . . . ' His eyes fixed on me for a second. 'And the Swan . . . '

The pause held for a moment, then it was over. 'Stone!' he said, abruptly. Silence. Then he reached a hand out, very slowly, and there was a block of pale stone in it, as if magicked out of air. 'Today's exercise is Mind of Stone. For those of you with us for the first time . . . it could not be simpler. Slow breaths, slow and slower. Every thought, think: *mind of stone*. Sit straight. Even the slightest move . . . ' He looked around. The genial flash in his eyes had gone, and there was his old stare, like a tunnel reaching back in darkness. 'I see you. *I see you*,' he said, sharp as the heron's stab. People round me stiffened. 'Let mind be hard and heavy. Nothing moves it. So you hold it, so . . . ' His voice was gentle, as he raised the stone at arm's length. He let go.

Crack. Now he smiled. At his feet the stone lay in two pieces. 'Stone rests. Falls. Breaks. Is all the same to mind of stone. Now, no more words. We are going for stone.' He was still, like a recording switched off with a click. The room was motionless around him. Was that all? I remembered my duel with the Stone Saints, trying to out-sit them. I remembered the agony of it, after half an hour. Now, there was no knowing how long I might have to hold this pose. And Antonin was watching, with those unfathomable eyes.

Time passed. Outside, the courtyard was already warm; as the sun angled up over the house it was suddenly hot, and humming. By the open window there was a bush with purple flowers, full of bees. It was a soothing sound, and it would have been sleepy if it hadn't been for Antonin. Watching. Time passed.

The humming was louder—not the gentle chorus of dozens of bees, but one note like a tiny version of the stonemason's saw. Moving only my eyes, I saw it coming down the line of sitting people—not a bee but a wasp, and a big one. It was interested in something, something about the people. Then I thought of breakfast. Porridge and syrup. Bread and jam.

There was Ange, with her tight little features and her perfect skin. I saw her tense as the wasp came closer. Right in front of her face it stopped. It hovered. I've known girls who look like her: this is the point where they jump up screaming, flapping their arms about until all their friends rush over and take care of them.

But Ange didn't. Maybe her lips tightened slightly but she didn't flinch as it dodged closer, away, closer again, then so close she must have felt its wing beat on her cheek. On her eyelids. Her lips. There must have been a trace of jam she hadn't licked away, because the thing landed, balanced on her lips, feeling this way and that, into the tender corner, buzzed its wings . . . and lifted off.

She hadn't moved a muscle. Nor did the Chinese-looking girl next to her. From face to face it came, and did anyone jump up, try to swat it or even turn their face away? Not one. Minds of stone, Antonin had said. I felt a kind of shiver. What am I getting into? I thought. Do I know what this place is really about at all?

But the wasp . . . The wasp had crossed the room and was working its way down the line on my side. Towards me. I couldn't do it. This was my first day; how could I be expected to? With a flash of anger I thought: he's done this on purpose, it's another test, he's conjured the wasp up out of nothing, like the stone. Five or six people down, the wasp came close, very slowly—buzz, stop, buzz . . .

Then a door opened somewhere, to one side and behind me. I couldn't see it, but the waft of cool air took the wasp and lifted it off, back towards the window, and I almost laughed with the relief. But there was another stillness in the room. Antonin had not moved, but I knew that someone else had entered and was watching—a quite different kind of watching—too.

98

It might have been my imagination, but I think everyone else had felt it. Whoever it was that had joined us, they neither took their place quickly, like a student, nor stepped into the centre of the room with Antonin. Instead, they came along the space behind me—slowly, stop, start, stop—down the narrow space between the sitting students and the wall. There was only the slight drag of a soft shoe on the carpet, then a pause, then the movement again, and I thought of the wasp, how it lingered on each face, prying into tender places. Whoever was there, right behind me now, I couldn't see, but the skin of my neck was tingling. I knew they were looking me over, with the kind of gaze you might use for a work of art, not a person.

It had to be Dominic. The collector, the dealer. It wasn't just the stone kind of statue he collected. He would be looking us over, his latest acquisitions: Amadeus and the Swan. Were we acceptable? What was he looking for? I couldn't—didn't want to—guess.

But I felt him looking. It wasn't like Antonin's gaze, that first time I'd sensed him without seeing, in the alleyway. Then, I'd felt the darkness in his eyes, I'd felt it like a cold wind. This was different. It was like a light touch, almost too light to feel—as if a question mark had drifted in on the breeze, like a dandelion seed, and hung over my head a moment . . . Just a moment . . . then the question mark moved on. I breathed again. My spine was aching from the effort not to turn and look. I felt him turn back, moving past me, pausing. And a student somewhere just to my left got to his feet. I felt the room relax as the door shut with a padded sound.

A minute later, Antonin suddenly clapped his hands. 'A short break,' he said crisply. 'Stretch your legs. Then to your places and work till lunchtime. Freestyle, no get-up. But *work*. I come round and observe. Remember,' he said as we got stiffly to our feet. 'I *see* you, anywhere and any time.' Then he was gone.

I looked for the empty space on my left. Who had it been? I hadn't noticed. I had the feeling that little things kept on happening in this place, in the corner of my eye, and when I looked there was nothing. I would have to keep my eyes peeled if I wanted to make sense of what was going on.

12

In the coffee room, Maisie was trying to catch my
eye. I was trying not to catch hers. I'd spotted Swan,
in the crush for the tea urn, and I pushed in right
behind her. 'Hi,' I said. 'What's up?'

'Hi.' She didn't turn round. All I could do was make
out her reflection in the stainless-steel urn.

'Come and sit down,' I pressed on, trying to sound
casual. 'Tell me what they did to *you* last night. I . . .'

'Not now.'

'Come on, I thought we were friends.'

'No!' She half turned now, but she didn't meet my
eye. 'Things are different here, Ni—I mean Amadeus.
Things are different, can't you see?'

'I don't see why . . .' Almost without thinking, I
touched her shoulder, like I'd done in the car park. And
she flinched away.

'Listen,' she said quietly. 'I'm doing fine. So are you.
Let's keep it that way.' She turned, and her eyes were
big, as if she was afraid. 'Please . . . I think someone
wants to talk to you.' And there was Maisie, peering
through the scrum, on tiptoe. *Hi*, I mouthed, without
encouragement, but when I looked back, Swan had
slipped away.

People were moving off for the next session of Work
already. It wasn't like school, where people drag the
breaks out for as long as they can get away with. To be the
last one out, I guessed, was not the thing to do. But as I
came out in the courtyard they'd all gathered in a little

101

crowd, as if some kind of show was starting. There was an expectant silence, then a hollow whirr, click, clock . . .

Something was waddling out with stiff steps on the cobbles. 'Look,' said Maisie, 'one of Albie's automatons. He's brilliant. It's part of his act—comes on as Einstein—Albie, get it?—kind of mad inventor . . . ' The others were clustering in already and we pushed in for a better view. Albie had come out of the stonemason's workshop, rather solemnly carrying a wooden bundle in his arms. He'd set it down in the middle of the cobbles, as carefully as you would a real toddler, balancing it upright on its paddle feet. It had a blank puppet face—two holes for eyes, a cut grin. He cranked a handle, and it made a clockwork sound. Antonin leaned in the doorway, his head on one side; Albie stepped back as the wooden child jerked and shuffled, clicked and jerked again. It began to jolt its way round in an arc—the two legs weren't quite in sync. It had done almost a full circle when it slowed and whirred and settled down again. There was a ripple of applause, and Albie looked at us, then at the darkened doorway where Antonin leaned. His gaze was dark as ever, and he had not smiled.

Antonin came out slowly, into the hush in the courtyard. He walked round the wooden child once, then felt its arm, its neck joint. He caught hold of a leg and rattled it. Something must have given way. With a cold look, Antonin set the thing back on its feet and it keeled over sideways, not quite falling, with one leg askew. The eyeholes and the grin looked stupid now, or insolent. With one sharp movement Antonin slapped the thing straight in the face; it fell flat on its back, its head knocked sideways.

There was a moment's hush. I looked at Albie. He wasn't looking at the automaton, but at Antonin's face, and for a moment I thought he was about to burst—to shout or laugh or cry. But he didn't. That was the shocking thing. He waited, with his head bowed and his face gone deathly pale, till Antonin turned his eyes away. Then Albie picked up the felled automaton, like a mechanical thing himself, and stumped away.

'Is he all right?' I said to Maisie. A couple of the others had gone after Albie, as soon as Antonin had moved off. Maisie nodded, and we followed them.

Inside the workshop it was dark, and there were several voices all together. One was sobbing—Albie. He must have just got out of sight, then crumpled. Now he was huddled on a pile of sacking, with his knees bent up and hands across his face, and shuddering. Laura-Lee was cradling his head; the others gathered close, soothing him, muttering the little sounds you might do to a small beaten child.

Bit by bit, through the sobs, I made out the story. He'd been on the street since he was thirteen, running from some stuff at home, you know the kind of thing . . . And half the group were nodding: yes, they did. Suddenly I felt like a tourist here. What did I know about it, with my little family tiff in my nice home, and my spat of bad temper about Malcolm's car? It felt wrong to be listening in. Now Albie was talking about the drugs he'd been doing, things I'd only heard of, and how as soon as the going got tough the mates had vanished and he was out there on his own. Again, the heads were nodding round him, people were muttering little comforts—yes, they knew—and he was crying freely. He'd never have made it, he was saying, if he hadn't been here, in the Place, with all his friends around him, and they must always be there for him, he was sobbing, please, please, please.

I was close now and Laura-Lee sensed me behind her. As she turned, for a terrible moment I thought she was going to tell me to leave. But no, she met my eyes and nodded as if, yes, she knew I'd understand.

As we came back into the light of the courtyard, Albie was almost silent. I looked at Maisie. 'Why . . . ?'

'He hasn't been here long. Takes time to toughen up.'

'No, I mean Antonin. Why did he *do* that?'

Maisie stopped and turned with a small puzzled frown. 'Because it wasn't good enough,' she said, as if that was the obvious answer. She put her hand on my sleeve. 'I told you,' she said. 'You need to understand about Antonin. They won't miss us at Work for five minutes. Come with me.'

There was a binder full of clippings, on newsprint the colour of tea. Maisie sat me down in the Cool Room, then brought it out from a hidden bookcase like a holy relic. Most of the text was in French, with some others that looked like Russian or Polish, with maybe an Indian language or two. The dates were clear, though—through from the early Fifties to an abrupt stop in May 1968. I recognized the photographs by people's beds. There were other pictures too: black-and-white or early colour that had faded unevenly, with all the red shades gone, leaving sometimes just a block of bluish background round a washed-out face but you could never fail to recognize the eyes. They were not sunken yet; he was tall, svelte, you could almost say handsome, but there was something in him that looked old, as if he'd always been practising to be what he was today. *Antonin Asch,* one headline said, *Mime Suprême ou Agent Provocateur?*

'That was the Communist paper,' said Maisie. 'They called him a dangerous anarchist. Think of that! Of course,' she dropped her voice, 'he'd go wild if he knew we kept this old stuff. But heck, it's important that new

104

people like you know just who this guy is. I mean, you don't have to speak French to get the gist of it. He was news. He knew everybody, actors, writers, all the Surrealists, the Existentialists, the Theatre of the Absurd . . . Look, there he is with Jean-Paul Sartre. And you know what, he didn't give a damn. He walked out of *Waiting For Godot* shouting that there was too much action.' That should have been a joke; she wasn't laughing. 'That's when he issued his manifesto about the Theatre Of Immobility.'

'Some guy . . . !' I said, sincerely. Every photograph, whether he was in white-face, like a clown, or made up like a skeleton or a cannibal chief, there were those eyes, those pits of dark. They gave me vertigo. 'But he's a bully, isn't he?'

She looked at me as if I'd started speaking a different language. 'What do you mean?'

'Out there, in the courtyard. I mean . . . '

'He's got high standards. What do you expect? We're here to be the *best*. He is a genius, after all.' She was shaking her head as she spoke, sort of not believing I could be so thick. 'Nobody bullies anybody here. We could walk out any time we liked.'

'But nobody does. Hob said . . . '

'He's another one to steer clear of,' Maisie put in. 'Take my advice.' Then she suddenly beamed. 'Trust us. Just believe in the Work. We all do.' She leaned closer. 'And no secrets, now. We share everything here. I just know you'll belong.'

'Can I see the next folder?' I said, to change the subject.

'That's all,' said Maisie.

'But . . . that's only 1968.'

'That's when he . . . stepped aside from history.' She looked at me as if I ought to understand. 'OK . . . ' She

105

reached down from the shelf a dusty lump of a book, the kind of thing nobody touches in the school reference library. She flicked through the pages. 'There . . .'

Asch, Antonin . . . There was a third of a column, in tiny print. His dates, the names of his productions . . . but I was skimming to the end. *His later work became increasingly obscure and unsettling. In 1968 following a shocking incident, he was committed to an asylum . . .*

'That's the establishment view,' said Maisie. 'You have to read between the lines.'

. . . *where he is believed to have stayed until his death (date unknown).*

She was watching my face. 'Hang on,' I said. 'It says here . . .'

'I know, I know. The asylum . . . that was where Dominic found him. Can you imagine that?' Her voice hushed to a whisper. 'No one knew who he was. He hadn't talked to anyone for thirty years.'

'Dominic . . . ? It doesn't say anything about that . . .'

'It was sort of unofficial. Dominic fixed it. As far as the records go, Antonin died. Oh, and he likes it that way. He says, *I like it, being dead* . . .' She laughed, and I tried to laugh with her.

'Maisie,' I said, 'what was the *shocking incident*?'

'Ah,' she waved her hand dismissively. 'When you're a genius . . . people just don't understand. They never do.'

I was glad of the practice session, when we caught up with the others. I needed air, and got it, because this time we were working on the terrace. People had ranged themselves along the gravel, some of them in window-niches, some using the low wall, and even in their everyday clothes they had frozen into statues by the time I arrived. I found a place, and went into my Mozart, trying to think of the tune, all calm and limpid, because the pictures in my head were swirling round and round. The meditation, and those few snatched words with Swan, then the stuff in the courtyard, Albie, and the history of Antonin. It was all coming at me too fast. I needed time to stand and think.

And that was what I had. It was a warm day, but a soft breeze came up from the lakeside, bringing the smell of cut grass and the sound of distant ducks. It couldn't be that bad, could it? I mean, I could be eking out my last twenty pence on coffee in the drop-in, with the Tin Man and the other losers who would give their eye teeth to be here. And what was so terrible anyway? Sure, Antonin was fierce, but now he was moving from statue to statue, head on one side, with a word of advice here and there. Every now and then he would adjust someone's posture, rather gently, as far as I could see. And there was Albie, back at work as Einstein: he didn't seem to have hard feelings. There was Swan, by the steps, going into her clockwork pirouette as gracefully as I'd ever seen her do it. She was fitting in, all right. And breath by breath I felt my heartbeat slowing. I'd been getting worked up. Maybe if I just relaxed a little . . . There was something peaceful in this statue business after all.

Now the sunlight was shifting so my shadow slid around me, and the glitter of the lake came through the little pillars that edged the terrace, and when I glanced sideways, there was Ange near the edge, with the sunlight behind her and stray wisps of thistledown blowing up and round, so for a moment I could almost think I saw the shape of angel wings.

I glanced back, and jumped. There was Antonin, straight in front of me, motionless. How he'd appeared, without a sound, on the gravel was beyond me. For a moment he watched me with those deep-back-in-the-

107

darkness eyes, and I braced myself for the explosion—some cutting remark, some public humiliation, some scorn.

'Not easy to be Mozart without music,' he said. 'Best you go and fetch your little whistle.' And he smiled.

I didn't hurry. Time was feeling different now, and I paused at the foot of the stairs. Something bright had caught my eye—a postcard drawing-pinned to the notice board. It was creased in the corner where people had bent it to see the other side. Poster-paint-blue sea, that's what it pictured, and a white arc of beach, and palm trees, with a few white villas low down by the water's side. *Mauritius*, the stamp read. The writing was in purple felt pen, in a rounded girlish script. *This is the Big Time all right,* it said. *Brilliant weather. Hot hot HOT! Big hugs to Laura-Lee and all of you. Miss you masses. Love you lots.* There was a little heart over the *i* of the name at the bottom: *Gloria*.

'That's what it's about. Fame and fortune!' It was Hob's voice, from behind me. I wheeled round. He was crouched motionless on the turn of the thick wooden banister, like a carved imp. Either I'd just walked straight past him or he'd moved into position behind me without a sound.

'What are you doing there?'

'Working, of course.' He did his rubber-faced grin. 'Tops of walls, ledges, parapets, anywhere high up. It's the gargoyle thing,' he said. 'Only really works if I'm looking down.'

'Who's this?' I said, flicking the postcard. 'One of the Old Girls?' I turned back to Hob, and he was gone.

'We call them graduates.' I spun back. He was in a little niche, almost beside me, where a real statue might have been.

'How do you do that?' I said.

'Practice. You just watch the other person and you

108

move when they move. Harder of course in a crowd.'
He jumped down onto the floor. 'They call me Mister
Behind-You—like in the pantomime: *He's be-hind you!* Old
Gloria, now . . . ' He flicked the card. 'She was quite a
stunner. No surprise when she was Picked. Everyone knew
she'd go far.' He giggled. 'The other girls hated her.
Jealous as cats.'

I thought of Swan's voice: *We aren't on the same side.
We're rivals.* Was that it? Was that why she was ignoring
me now? I wanted to find her and shake her and say: We
are on the same side. We *are*! What about the moments in
the courtyard, in the van?

'Don't worry, you'll have your chance,' said Hob. 'You
fancy yourself in Mauritius?'

'What about you? You sound cool about it.'

He narrowed his eyes, though the grin did not waver.
'I'm just fine,' he said. 'I like it where I am. But you go for
it if you want to. They'll expect you to.'

Then he was halfway up the stairs, although I'd hardly
blinked. 'If you want to keep up with your friend,' he said,
'you'll need to work overtime.'

'What friend?'

'The Swan. Oh, come on, you and her, it's pretty
obvious, to anyone who looks.' He jumped up on his
banister, and was motionless again. 'And people do.
They're looking all the time.'

'Thanks.' The expression on his face was stone still.
Was he laughing at me, or was this a warning? I couldn't
tell.

'Just keep your eyes open,' he said, through the grin.
'It pays to keep your wits about you in this place.'

13

'Keep your heads up. Hold your abs in. Knee up, one and two and . . . Yeah. That's it. Now thrust! *Yo-hey*!' The music speeded up a gear, and louder. It was tacky disco stuff, forgotten big hits from the 80s: I could have been back in the doorway of the Sports Centre gym where Mum went when she decided to stop mouldering and take herself in hand. Except now I was out on the floor with all the others, and pounding away. If I'd felt like scoffing, an hour of the stuff had wiped the smile off my face. I was sweating and aching, and still the same half dozen tunes came round, and the voice from the video kept on, healthy, Californian, relentless. Worst of all, when I glanced sideways, there was Maisie, and Swan, and Albie, with their heads up and the same bright smile as the woman on the screen, pounding on.

'Now jump. And turn. Yo-hey! Now cool it, cool it.' The music tailed off into New Age whale song. 'We'll take a breather,' said the voice. 'And stretch. No sitting down. Keep moving.' I looked around. I couldn't see anyone else who was out of breath like me, though Swan was a bit pink. They weren't just playing at it, all these pretty people; if they looked good, they were going to keep it that way. I thought of Mr Bunce, the gym teacher we all hated at my old school; I'd have liked to see him here, to suffer.

Laura-Lee had been right, that first evening: this place wasn't a holiday. Four days in now, I was getting a feel for

110

the routine. There was practice—the Work—and the things you did to keep yourself in trim for Work. Oh, and there was the housework—cooking, cleaning, washing up, all the things I'd never done much of at home. Here, I was kind of glad of them, all but toilet duty, that is, because you got to stand round with a bunch of others doing ordinary things. Sometimes no one would mention their Work for, oh, a whole half hour. Sometimes after lunch people lounged on the grass, laughing and chatting, and the place had a time-off feel, but at two o'clock sharp, they were all on their feet, on their way to a session. There was nobody making them do it. Antonin wasn't in sight. Sometimes I thought it was the thought of Success that kept them at it; sometimes it seemed that life here was enough, just being with each other, doing what they did.

From the whispers I picked up, no one had a life outside you'd want to send your worst enemy back to. Antonin had done his choosing well. As for me, there was no danger of Malcolm catching up with me here. And Mum? I'd send her a postcard one day—maybe one with a postmark from one of the wonderful places the star pupils, the Glorias, got to. Like everyone else, I'd glance at that card on my way past, and dream. At the end of the day we'd have a laugh and doss round in the Cool Room, but not for long. Come the evening, I'd be looking forward to bedtime when I could hit the sheets and be asleep.

I hardly had time to notice that we didn't get to be alone. Yes, there were the gardens and the woods, and no one said you couldn't wander. But the others didn't, and you just knew there'd be a certain look on their faces—just to say they'd noticed—if you did. You might think you'd get to think your own thoughts, quietly inside, while you were working, but try doing that when Antonin is watching. Worse, we were going to have Crit sessions, when everyone watched one of us, looking for the slightest falter. Antonin didn't bully us; he would stand, impassive. 'Any comments?' he would say, and everybody piled in. It was merciless. I thought of Albie, crumpled in the workshed like a broken puppet, and I wondered who else had crept off to sob in secret. I wasn't looking forward to the day I had my turn.

'Hi, there,' I said to Swan, as the aerobics class broke ranks. 'How's things?' It was starting to get to me, how every mealtime she just happened to be on some other table. At dinner I'd catch sight of her from behind, hair tucked behind her ears, and she would be talking, with four or five of them leaning towards her. Just for a moment I'd want to throw their chilli con carne in their faces. Why should she be the life and soul of the party for them and not for me?

Now, she didn't look at me. 'You've got to stop this,' she said in a flat voice. 'We've got new friends. We've got work to do.'

'I thought *we* were friends,' I said.

'Look,' she said. 'Look around you. All these guys and girls and . . . well, nothing . . . going on?'

'Hang on, I didn't mean . . . '

'No, no . . . ' For a moment we both fluffed our lines. I could feel myself blushing. 'I mean,' she said, 'not getting, like, separate from the others.'

'That's a rule, is it? No drink, no drugs, no smoking, no having friends. Who says? Antonin?'

'Nobody *says*. It's how it *is*. Nick . . . ' She blushed. She'd said it—*Nick*, not Amadeus. 'You've got to fit in,' she whispered. 'You'll get in trouble if you don't.' Almost quicker than I had time to notice, she'd caught hold of my hand and squeezed it and let go. 'Look after yourself, won't you? Please.'

'I don't care what we're *supposed* to do . . . '

112

'Well, I do. I care what happens to you. I care about *you*.'

For a moment my breath seemed to catch in my chest. 'Well, then . . . Let's . . .'

'No!' she cut in. 'That's why we mustn't see each other. Don't you understand?'

'Yes, but . . . No . . .'

And before I could think what to say there was a hubbub, over by the window. First there were one or two people by it, pointing, then there was a crush of them, jostling to get a view. 'Look,' called someone, 'guess who's back?' From behind, I couldn't see what they were looking at, and Swan and I were just like the rest of them, pushing our way through. 'He didn't last long!' crowed someone. Somebody chimed in, 'Who's the big star now?' Then everyone was talking at the same time, laughing, calling to each other, half to whoever it might be outside: 'Reckon he's coming back to join us mortals?' 'Get him in here, get his flab into shape!' Someone rapped on the window and everyone who could reach pressed their faces to the pane and leered.

'Come on, we're here to work!' called Laura-Lee. As the crowd broke up I pushed through and I got a glimpse. Over the courtyard somebody's back, someone in a ragged costume, was just disappearing through the archway. There was something slouching and defeated in the way he walked.

'Hi, welcome to Part Two of the PowerPlan Program!' came the video voice and the beat locked back in. 'This time we're gonna take you further. Are you ready? Yo-hey! Here we go!'

'What was that all about?' I said to Ange, when we broke for tea. Swan had made herself scarce; we didn't have another chance to speak.

'Serves him right,' said Ange, and her pretty little features tightened. 'You saw him the other day. Thinking he knows best. Always telling us how *he* was going to make it, how Dom had his eye on *him*, what *Antonin* had told him—him, him, him!'

'Sorry,' I said. 'Who?'

'Mattheus, of course. Well, he's had his chance. And blown it, by the looks of it.'

I must have been looking dense. 'You know,' she said. 'He was Picked. And now he's back.'

'So?' I said.

'He blew it. Didn't make the grade.' She smiled thinly. 'They're right: he's getting flabby. Spends all his time in front of the mirror, grooming his silly Pan costume. Get fat, Dom won't look at you. He's got taste, Dom has. He's got contacts in New York, Tokyo, you name it. Why should he bother about a jumped-up little berk like Matty?' Then she was looking away; someone had caught her attention.

'Did you say Matty?' I called after her, as we surged into the dining room. But she wasn't listening. The hair, the beard, the Pan costume . . . Of course. I'd only heard the name once but it stuck in my mind. I could hear the slight hush in the Stone Saints' voices. *A real class act*, they'd said, *before he Went* . . . Was that what they'd be saying in the drop-in now, about me and the Swan? Why hadn't I spotted it earlier? Mattheus was Matty the Pan.

He would have to appear, some time. This was the guy the Stone Saints had talked about. Even the Tin Man said he had a sort of gift, and the Tin Man was the most jealous guy I'd ever met . . . until I reached the Place, at least. The way some of them talked behind each other's backs here made the Tin Man sound like a kind uncle. Next moment they would have their arms around each other, one big family again. I guess that's just how drama

114

people are, but back in Young Stagers we had homes to go to, and school, and the rest of our lives. Not here: Work was everything. And yet . . . it was a long time now since anywhere had felt like home, and . . . Well, when I saw the others in one of their group hugs, I wanted to be in there. Sometimes I was. Some nights, I'd wake and wonder what would happen if one day they turned round to me: *You don't belong here. Go away.* I imagined myself like a stray cat, out in the dark, scratching at the door with the lights and the voices inside it, and my own cat voice, like Albie's that day, crying *Please, please, please* . . .

I was learning things, too, the way they'd said I would. I was almost not an outsider any more. At least, I knew about Antonin. But Dominic? *Dom, Dom* . . . The name was always in the background, like a sort of muffled drum. When I tried asking her outright, Laura-Lee was vague. He came and went, she said. On business. Galleries, she said, when I pressed on. And private collectors—he had contacts everywhere. She was getting impatient already. I wanted to know more. Was he part of the community? 'Of course not,' Laura-Lee shook her head.

'But he's the one who Picks people, isn't he?' I said. 'He picked Mattheus . . . What happens then?'

'You'd do better to think about the Work,' she said, 'you're very new,' and turned away.

The more I asked, and the more I wasn't told, the more I thought: I want a good talk with Matty the Pan.

He didn't appear to eat that evening. He wasn't upstairs or in the Cool Room. After supper the others collapsed in front of *EastEnders*, almost like a real family. I'd have liked to be with them, but I slipped away. There were a couple of beds that looked unslept-in, and on the wall above one of them was a statuing shot that had to be him—beard, horns, and shaggy from the waist down: the god Pan. Where had he got to? Where would I go if I wanted to be on my own? In the gardens, outside? As I thought it, I realized that a breath of air was what I wanted anyway.

The evening light was blurry with a thin mist. Moistness settled on my skin and was cool. There was a far faint sound, nowhere in particular, that might have been wind in the trees, but must have been the rush of water in the culvert. For a moment, though, it was the sound of sea, all round us, cutting me off from the world outside.

I scanned the courtyard, then the lawns, then made for the walled gardens. Pale or blotchy marble faces gazed out of the murk as I half tiptoed, half ran, by. When I looked back, the house was vague; the windows of the upper storey looked down as blank as ever. And there he was, opposite the Venus de Milo, in an alcove of box hedge, with his goat's hindquarters and small horns, and pipes in his hand.

He had a frosting of dew already on his shaggy pants. Though there was leathery paint on his naked top half, I could see goose pimples showing through. 'Matty?' I said. Even at a distance I could see him shivering. His hand was shaking and his eyes twitched to and fro. 'I've heard of you,' I said. 'I know the Stone Saints. Remember?'

'Leave me alone.' He said it through his teeth.

'I need to talk to you,' I said. 'Look, it's cold, it's raining. Why not give it a break?'

He turned his head suddenly, and his eyes were blazing. 'Beat it.' He dropped his panpipes, and jumped down to scrabble for them. 'He knows I'm here. He'll be watching.'

'It's dark,' I said. 'Anyway, Antonin's inside.'

'Not Antonin—Dominic! He's the one that matters. He's got the key. I can show him, just you watch me. This time . . . ' He scrambled back on to the plinth and raised his face towards the house. 'This time I'm going for stone.'

'You're freezing,' I said, taking a step nearer. His whole body tensed, one arm drawn back. The others might say he was flabby; I saw muscle. 'Beat it,' he said again. 'Try to stop me, I'll kill you.'

'OK, OK . . .'

His eyes stared through me. 'Stone,' he was muttering as I backed away. 'Going. Going for stone.'

Back by the house, I looked up. A few windows were lit. Which was Swan's? I wanted to tell someone what I'd just seen, but in my mind I heard the mocking laughter at the window. They weren't going to cluster round Matty and comfort him like they'd done Albie. He was out; he'd broken some rule of the place, or maybe they were just jealous, because he'd been with Dom. I didn't know why Swan should be any different, but I knew, I thought I knew, she had to be. And maybe it wasn't Matty the Pan I wanted to tell her about; maybe I wanted to tell her about me.

I looked up at the house. As I watched, an outline appeared in a window, just for as long as it takes for somebody to part the curtains, lean their face close to the glass, see nothing much and turn away. It could have been anyone, but as I crept into the hall, I couldn't help the picture coming back and back again, with a little more detail, her face, or the tilt of her head like those computer-enhanced versions of blurry CCTV images you get on the news sometimes, after a bomb blast or some particularly nasty crime.

Sometimes you can't imagine how you're going to sleep . . . and then you do. I couldn't join the others in the Cool Room now. I went to bed and lay there staring at the ceiling, and the last thought I remember was *I've got to think this through* . . .

I was out on the terrace. The lake was like metal and the sweep of the lawns was unbroken but I knew there'd have to be a ha-ha—the kind of sunken wall rich people used so as not to spoil their view. *Oh, there'll always be walls, you count on it. Keep the likes of us out.* Dad had said that on some family outing and Mum told him off. 'You're always so bloody negative,' she said. Ha-has never sounded like a joke to me. In the dream the ghostly lord and lady sat, taking tea, and Dad was with them, slightly see-through, too, and there was music, crisp and tinkling. Mozart. It was coming from his statue, in white clothes, lifting a white recorder to its lips, and its face was as white as the moonlight and expressionless but sad, sad, and I knew it couldn't speak and it was me.

I woke thinking: How long till they notice that I only know one tune? Will I be tried and found wanting, ditched, like Matty the Pan?

It was early, and light. None of the others was stirring. Matty wasn't back. I picked up my clothes and tiptoed to the door. It had rained in the night, the grass and trees outside were glistening in the early sun and the scene could have been beautiful, if I had stopped to admire it. I went down the steps into the sculpture garden, round the corner of the box hedge, to the plinth. It was empty.

He had fallen in the flower bed, full length, on his face. He lay limp and shivering. I crouched beside him. As I turned him on his back his head rolled over, and his eyes were open, but rolled up almost beneath their lids and not looking at me. I put my hand on his forehead; it had the oily feel of stage paint, but cold. His lips moved slightly and I remembered once, on an adventure holiday on Snowdon, I'd seen someone in the second stage of exposure—not unconscious yet, but going vague. The leader had taken one look and sent someone to run for

Mountain Rescue; leave it an hour, they'd really be in trouble, she said.

I pulled off my sweater and wrapped it around him. Then he seemed to blink and take me in. 'It's OK,' I said. 'You'll be OK.'

He raised a trembling hand and groaned. 'I'll get help,' I said. That's when he grabbed me by the collar, pulling me towards him, struggling to speak.

'No!' He forced the words out. 'No help.' He fell back, still gripping my collar. 'It was the rain. If he'd seen me . . .'

'Who? Antonin?'

'No! Him. *Him!*'

'You mean Dominic?'

'So near . . . Nearly chosen. You know what that means? You don't. Too new.' He pulled me close. 'Only thing worth having,' he breathed. 'You see that, nothing, nothing else will do.'

I jerked free. 'I'm getting help.' I went up the steps three at a time. By the time we got back to the garden, there was my sweater, crumpled, wet with dew. Of Matty the Pan, there was no trace.

14

'**B**ut where's he got to?' This was breakfast. People were spooning out cornflakes just like any morning, as if nothing had happened. I'd caught sight of Laura-Lee by the tea urn, and I cornered her.

'Where is he?' I said. 'Shouldn't we . . . well, mount a search or something? Shouldn't we tell Dom . . . or Antonin? Who's in charge here?'

'Nobody's *in charge*,' said Laura-Lee. 'We're all in it together. And if someone doesn't fit in . . . if they want to walk out on it, well, that's their decision.'

'But . . . ' I said.

'I wouldn't concern yourself,' she cut in, 'if I were you. I really wouldn't. The fact that you crept out looking for him . . . Well, you're new here. We can let that go.'

'Aren't you worried? He was in a bad way. Really bad.'

She turned to me sharply. 'Not too bad to walk away,' she said. 'Look, we don't keep people locked up. If they want to go, they go.'

'But Dom . . . ' I said. 'Shouldn't someone tell him? After all . . . ' But Laura-Lee just moved away.

Hob was there beside me. 'Leave it,' he said, sidelong. 'It won't do you any good.'

'I don't get it,' I said, as we sat down. 'Everyone bangs on about how we've got to work hard and be serious. Then someone does and look what happens. They hate him for it.'

120

Hob shrugged. 'You never been in a drama group?' He gave a kind of smile, half apologetic. 'You must admit, he was a bit of a pain. Nobody likes that.'

I couldn't quarrel with that. Besides, Hob was OK. I hadn't heard him bitching, like the others. And when it was all luvvie-hugs, he'd be there, but not quite in the thick of it. 'Tell me,' I kept my voice down, 'why are you here?'

'Why not?'

'Oh, come on. Everyone else is so . . . intense. Sort of desperate. Like Matty the Pan. Like Albie.'

He didn't turn. If anyone had been watching, they'd have thought we were just passing the time of day. 'And what about you?'

'That's different.'

'Is it?' Now he looked at me, straight. 'Everybody's got a story. Mostly, we don't talk about them much. Like you.'

'OK,' I said. 'I had family trouble. It sort of went downhill from there.'

'Have trouble with the law?'

'No.' There was something in the way he asked. 'Did you?'

'I just needed to . . . disappear for a while,' he said. 'I've got a talent for it. Suits me just fine that we're sort of incommunicado here. Free bed and breakfast, nice place, nice people. Almost like a holiday.'

'Oh, yeah? And Matty? I saw the state he was in. Something had really got inside him, something really deep.'

'So? He had his big audition, and he blew it.'

Yes, I'd seen kids biting the carpet and blubbering, even in auditions for school pantos, but . . . 'It was like he was crazy. Right out of his mind. What does Dom do with people when he picks them?'

'Maybe you'll find out.'

'I think I'd rather not. You're not busting a gut to be picked, are you?'

'No comment,' Hob said. 'Oh, but your friend the Swan . . . ' He leaned closer. 'She wants it. Wants it too much. I'd warn her, or she'll end up like Matty the Pan.'

I checked everywhere, even the ha-ha. (My dream had been right—there was one.) Slipping out of breakfast, I'd gone down the damp grass quickly; my feet were soaking but I didn't want to make noise on the gravel. The ditch was all clogged with brambles, but he wasn't there. I went round the gardens, stopping to poke the dripping bushes. What if he'd just crawled off and was lying there, only feet away? I went through the gardens one by one, down at last to the Sculpture Garden: the pond with the god with the conch . . . The grotto . . . There was a lion head in a low wall, with the fountain trickling from its jaws. The plinth where he'd been was very empty. What hit me with a kind of aftershock was the certainty: someone was watching me. I looked; there was no one there. The house, with its blank windows, was still in a swathe of mist. There was only the stone lion, watching, and Venus de Milo staring with her little borehole eyes.

I crept in at the back of the room. The session had started dead on time; that was Antonin's way. Every couple of days, he'd give a demonstration—not in the get-up I'd seen in Maisie's album but in plain black, as though the mime artist's costume had become him, and he'd become it. The powdery grey of his face was just how he looked all the time.

I'd hurried up back from the gardens, and found the

door open a crack, and slipped in among the people standing round the edge of the room. Luckily, Antonin's back was to the audience.

He wasn't still, but moving very, very slowly. Nothing athletic, but I remembered watching Swan that first day in the street—how I'd seen the tension in her calf-muscles quivering. And there she was, over in the corner, looking up at the master with a concentration almost as fierce as his own. That was the difference between us: if I'd been watching Antonin, and she'd crept in, I'd have known in an instant. Now, the light from the window fell sideways across her face, making it pale and mask-like, with her eyes in shadow. For a moment, it could have been Antonin's eerie dark stare looking out of her eyes.

She wants it too much. That's what Hob had said. *Warn her.* But how could I? We mustn't even be seen talking. I remembered the flash in her eyes when she'd told me to keep away from her.

'Contr-r-rol . . . ' His voice was slow as the movement, and as harsh as the creak of a door. 'You feel the pain, and you contr-r-rol . . . And all the time . . . the mind of stone.' He was moving so slowly that I could barely see it, but if I looked away (to glance at Swan, say, to see if she'd noticed me) when I looked back his posture was different.

'When you are still, like stone,' his voice grated on, 'the skin has eyes.' I once saw a film about ninjas, how they train them in the darkness, learning to feel what's around them with senses the rest of us don't have. I remembered that feeling by the abbey, how I'd let things round me seep into my brain. 'My skin sees who comes late . . . ' said Antonin, and paused. 'Who looks away . . . Who blushes now . . . ' Several of the others glanced in my direction. In case Antonin's extrasensory apparatus hadn't picked me up, they'd give him a clue.

123

Then suddenly he clapped his hands and laughed, and everyone jumped as if there'd been a small explosion. 'We are too tense,' he said. 'You all need to relax. We have a little holiday!' And he stepped, almost skipped, to the door and we followed, as if he was the Pied Piper and we were the children of Hamelin, or the rats.

'Professor Einstein!' he cried, in the courtyard, and looked towards the workshop door. For a moment nothing happened, then with a shuffle and click a figure tottered forwards. It was child-size, but with a small moustache, and it was made of wood—another of Albie's automata, this time with his own face on it. I held my breath as I thought of the last time, of Antonin's merciless judgement . . . and of Albie's voice that first morning saying *Please, please, please*. But this time it walked in a straight line, teetering a little on the cobbles, then getting its balance. Every ten steps it stopped, and bowed a little from the waist, then balanced upright and teetered on. The third time it bowed Antonin raised his hands and began applauding, and we all joined in, and Albie came out of the workshop, glowing with smiles, and we all applauded him too.

Then it was a little holiday. We lazed out on the terrace and sprawled on the lawn. The mist had cleared, as if on cue, and the sunshine on the lawns and trees was like a new coat of paint. Not for the first time I tried to remember last night's panic, or the strangeness in the mist before breakfast. It was part of my dream. It just didn't seem true. Surely any moment now Matty the Pan would come walking out of the bushes and say, 'Sorry, don't know what got into me,' and we'd all hug him and he'd be all right? As I looked around I thought of the students at the sixth form college that I'd never got to. I used to see them out on the grass at lunchtimes when I was on my way to the playing field from school; I'd felt like a kid in my uniform, and I'd thought: that's the life for me. And wasn't *this* that life, only better? Even Antonin lay on the grass and let the sunlight warm him. I was looking round for Swan when the French windows opened and somebody brought out a hamper full of ice creams—courtesy of Dom, it seemed, who'd got wind of the holiday. I couldn't quite remember what I'd been so worried about, so uptight, after all.

'Crit time!' called Laura-Lee, and we all trooped back into the long room. It was afternoon now, and we'd been out in the garden, out in our full get-up for the first time, practising in earnest. It was hard not to look at the others as you practised, but I guessed that must be part of the test. I recognized the postures and the movements, but suddenly these weren't the people I had breakfast with. There was a picture-book angel who had to be Ange, and a rather terrifying Amazon who could only be Maisie. Laura-Lee (I should have guessed it) was a sort of mermaid-like Lorelei. Swan wasn't in sight, but I knew her costume well enough. Hob appeared here and there, perched on a wall or gateway, like a know-all little gargoyle, and next time you looked he'd be gone. I'd dusted off my Mozart kit and done my best to turn to stone.

It was peaceful at first, the kind of thing old anglers must be after, under their big green umbrellas, sitting for whole days on end. Even Antonin had sounded something like light-hearted as he stalked around us, scrutinizing each in turn. He'd thrown his arm around Venus De Milo's waist. 'Perfect!' he'd said. 'Perfect act, perfect woman!' And with that he'd stood on tiptoe to plant a kiss, not a peck but a real long wet smacker, on her marble lips. Then he left us for an hour or so, to do the hard part—go on with the Work not knowing whether anyone was watching or not. But gradually the peaceful feeling of the gardens settled over us, and I relaxed. It didn't feel like being watched, and when I got an itch at the back of my leg I glanced around, no one was looking, and I scratched it happily.

'Crit time!' Laura-Lee called, and half the sculptures in the garden stirred, and stretched, and trooped back up the hill.

Crits worried everyone. I knew the score: someone would be picked at random, and we'd watch, like vultures. Then came the free-for-all. It was all about the art, Laura-Lee would remind us, but it was hard to remember that when everybody turned on you. So we knew what to expect. Only this time as we tumbled in, back in our everyday clothes, we came in to face a blank white screen.

Lights went out; the screen flickered. I've seen crisper home videos, even the terrible ones Dad used to take on holiday. This one looked like something taken with a pin-hole camera, the crudest sort of experiment you do in science at school. The frames came at us like moths at a windscreen in a car at night, and at first I couldn't make out what we were meant to be seeing. Then I did. A statue. It was Mozart. It was me.

The audience tittered a little. I could see why. I looked stiff at first, then my eyes looked this way, then that. A quick glance, and my hand reached down, and scratched. The whole room burst into laughter; the camera jerked, the footage of the moment reeled by again, and this time the people round me laughed harder, and it wasn't funny. It was like those TV programmes where your family send in the moments that make you look a fool.

Now it was someone else, maybe a tremble or a stumble, but not much, and the audience simmered, waiting for

126

the next chance. Then it was Maisie: one false move and they erupted, with that hard-edged laughter. I glanced at Antonin. He was by the projector, and not laughing at all. For the half hour the performance lasted, he never stirred. Laura-Lee was beside him, as she often seemed to be, but when it came to her turn, even she bit her lip and tried to look away. One by one it went round; everyone had something, caught mercilessly and edited for effect. Everyone, it seemed, but Swan. Were they saving her for last? I waited, waited . . . then it was over. No Swan. Had she been perfect, or was someone doing her a favour? I glanced round, but I couldn't see her in the room.

As we trooped out, subdued, no one met anybody else's eyes. The holiday feeling was over. It wasn't getting back to work that bothered me; it was the sound of that laughter. Were we meant to be friends, or weren't we? I looked round for Hob, but when I tried to catch his eye he looked away. I knew what he might say—that I was no different. Hadn't I been laughing too? With a shiver I thought: this place, I'm part of it now. Or it's a part of me, which seemed worse. I tried to think of the normal things again—the breakfast cereal, the little family rows; I tried to think about exams, and fancying girls, and staying out later than Mum liked at parties; I tried to think about Mum and Malcolm, the ordinary so-what's-new step-parent thing. It all seemed like a lost world. I'd become a member of a different species.

It didn't even matter that I tumbled, suddenly, where the video footage had come from. I thought of the places I'd been, and the sight lines, and what was in the place to see me. Statues. That was crude enough, all those stone faces with their pinhole eyes. Another time, I might have been excited by working that out. Now, there was a weight in my mind as heavy as Antonin's mind-of-stone. I was part statue already. I'd read about religious cults, and

127

parents who pay to have their children kidnapped back and put through therapy. Even if I left this place today, all this would always be a part of me. No de-programming on earth would stop that being true.

'I wouldn't spend too much time with Hob,' said Ange.

This was said casually, as we peeled potatoes in a big steel bowl. How long had I spent talking to Hob? Two minutes at breakfast? Five minutes on the stairs the other day? But as I knew now, walls have ears and eyes.

'He's casual. And he's too fond of going off by himself. Skulking. Whispering in corners.' She cast a look at me. 'If he's got anything to say, why not say it to all of us?' I didn't say anything. 'I happen to know,' she said after a pause, 'that his attitude has been noticed.' She went on peeling, not meeting my eyes. 'And you needn't feel so special just because Antonin said *You have it.*' She waited for that to register. Who could have told her that? 'Having it's not enough, here. You've got to work. You've got to really *want* it. You've got to *believe* in it, if you really want to *get there.*'

'I want to get there, all right. I want to see Mauritius, you bet. I know what I want.' That was meant to please her, but a look passed over her face as if she'd already said too much.

'Hm. Like your friend, you mean?'

'Oh . . . Swan?' I tried to make it casual.

'*She's* ambitious, all right. She's desperate. Have you known her long?' That stopped me. Add it up—how many days had it been? But Ange knew the answer anyway. 'I thought not,' she said. 'You're different, you and her. I don't know what's in this for you, but she's been through Hell.'

'I thought we weren't supposed to talk about the past?'

'No need to talk. You've noticed her arms, then.' I looked away. I closed my eyes a moment and there was Swan's face in my mind. But her arms . . . ? Ange smiled, coolly. 'Take a look one of these days. You might get a glimpse of some of the things she's not telling you.' One of the guys poked his head round the door. 'Get a move on, you two. What are you doing with those spuds— polishing them?'

'OK,' I called back. Ange still had that smile on her face.

'Take a look,' she said again, 'when she gets back. If she does.'

'Back? Back from where?' When had I last seen Swan? In Antonin's class, that morning, yes. That felt days ago. Did I see her in the courtyard? On the terrace? In the garden? On the video? All the answers were No. Whatever Ange meant about Swan's arms, I didn't know or care. But where *was* she? 'Where is Swan?' I said.

Ange shrugged. I grabbed her sleeve. She pulled but I didn't let go. At last she turned to me, her lips thin, and her baby-blue eyes glittered with a kind of spite.

'Maybe she's getting her chance,' she said. 'Her go at stone. That's nice, isn't it?'

'What do you mean?' But the answer was there in my mind already, as heavy as stone. 'She's been Picked? Is that what you're saying? Tell me!'

Ange gave me a withering look. 'What Dom should see in her I can't imagine,' she said. 'But everybody knows that's what she's after. Not waiting her turn—taking every chance to get herself noticed. Everybody hates her in the girls' room.'

Then there was a scream—first one, then several people shouting. I heard chairs clattering and footsteps running, people calling to each other up the stairs. 'Quick, quick,' someone was shouting. I looked out of the scullery;

everyone had dropped what they were doing and were jostling with each other, making for the door. I came out in the courtyard with them, panting, and ploughed into the back of a small crowd, suddenly quite still. Through the archway there came the groundsman trundling something heavy in a wheelbarrow. It could have been a broken automaton like Albie's, but it wasn't. One arm dangled limp and wet over the side.

It was Matty the Pan, and the barrow was dripping— water, I think, more than blood. Then the whispers were being passed back and I tried not to think about the pictures they brought to my mind. Drowned, they said. In the water for hours. Hours, though they'd felt like days, when the rest of us had been eating ice cream on the terrace. While we'd been dressing up in our costumes, he'd been floating, face down. In the end they'd found him tangled like a piece of driftwood in the teeth of the sluice.

15

I think I panicked. Suddenly it was all too much—all the others throwing themselves into each other's arms, sobbing and wailing. It was too theatrical. I couldn't breathe. An hour earlier all I'd have heard about Matty the Pan was bitchy gossip; now he'd been everyone's best friend. People were trading the last time each of them had spoken to him, and the warning signs they'd spotted. 'Well, *I* . . .' they'd start, in low solemn voices. Even now, they were competing. 'Well, what he said to *me* . . . ' In a moment someone would ask who was the last one to see him alive and everyone would swivel round and look at me.

I couldn't breathe. I had to get away.

Round on the terrace, I leaned my head against cool stone, breathed deep and let the evening sounds wash over me. Then I remembered what the sound was, rushing water. The culvert. The grille. I could see the bent uneven teeth of it, some of them just breaking water and rusted to knife points, with foam riding up against it, and stuck leaves and bits of flotsam from the lake impaled. And Matty.

Had he crawled back there on purpose, to end where he'd been initiated, like me, on his first night in this place?

Then I was frightened in a new way. What had they done to him? What was this place doing to us all? That look I'd seen in Matty's eyes, last night—it was saying *If I can't get back*—back to whatever Dom had offered him—

131

I'd rather die. He couldn't see beyond these walls any more. And suddenly the stone walls, and the woods like walls behind them, all came closing in. I couldn't breathe. Where was the way out? I didn't even know that. So I panicked. I ran.

I avoided the gardens. Were the spy-hole cameras only in the Sculpture Garden, or were they everywhere? Were they only used for Work or were they scanning night and day? I played safe and kept to the shadows. All the lights of the house seemed to be on, throwing wedges of light down the lawns, so I ducked among the bushes. I merged with the shadows and became invisible. Every now and then I heard a sound, and froze.

I *had* to see out. I should have known, the first time I met Laura-Lee, outside the doss-house hotel, or in the Safe House, and saw that look in her eyes. I'd wondered then if she was from something religious. Maybe this wasn't so far from the truth after all.

There was the gate. And at last I got a grip and thought a practical thought. When we'd looked out of the van that first night, the steel bars opened by themselves. That meant there had to be surveillance cameras. As I watched, there was a flicker of lights as a car passed on the road outside, and I had this crazy urge to run over and press my face against the gate, just to see that ordinary scene. *We don't keep people locked up,* Laura-Lee had said. *If they want to go, they go.* Had that ever been true? Even if it had, would it still be true now, with a suspicious death on their hands? Maybe I could just walk to the gate and wave and it would open.

Maybe . . . but does it sound likely to you?

If I ran to the gate I could shout, I could wave through the bars; someone might see me and pull over . . . Sure! I only had to think the thought to know it wouldn't happen. And even if it did, and a car pulled up, what would I

132

say? I could see myself babbling, wild-eyed, and then Antonin or Dom or a groundsman coming over, all sweet reason. I'm sorry for the inconvenience, madam, they would say, but some of our patients are very disturbed.

Maybe I was some sort of crazy, to find myself here? Of my own free will, too. And I'd never even found out where the nearest village was, or asked the Place's real name.

I had to think clearly. I edged around the driveway, closer to the house, until I saw what I'd expected: there was a small hut, almost a sentry box, where someone must sit on duty. I angled round for a view of the window. There was a light on, but I couldn't see him in there, and as I crept closer I saw the door at the back was open. With the hubbub at the house, maybe he'd gone to see?

This was a chance. If I moved fast, I could be inside that hut in seconds. I could find the closed-circuit TV. I could find the switch that worked the gates. I could be out of those gates before anyone knew what was happening. All I had to do was move; don't hesitate.

I hesitated.

I was ready to run. I was thinking, *Three minutes and all this will be behind me: no more Antonin with his crazy guru games, no more bitchiness, no more invisible Dom, no more . . .*

. . . no more Swan.

And I paused. Oh my God, I had forgotten Swan. She was back in there. All these days of watching for her, and I'd panicked at the sight of Matty. All my big scenes about *I'm your friend, I'll be there for you . . .* and I'd just run.

Swan had gone with Dom: Ange had as good as said it. Picked. And what did that mean? The one person who could have told me was Matty the Pan. I closed my eyes, and saw the rushing water, and the rusty grille. I saw a body with the rest of the discarded rubbish. In my mind's eye, it wasn't Matty, it was Swan.

I'd like to say that I made a snap decision. No. What I did was: I hesitated. Run to get help? Or go back to find her? And a moment later there was the blink of a flashlight, and one of the groundsmen came down the drive from the house. That settled it. I doubled back to the house to find Swan.

And there she was. As I slipped back into the hallway she was just at the bottom of the stairs, hurrying somewhere. 'Hey!' I called, and she turned a moment.

'There you are,' she said. 'This way.' And that was all. She was out of the front door, and I followed, feeling foolish. What had I thought I was going to do—burst in and rescue her from something? But Swan was OK. She hadn't been Picked; Ange had been wrong. I came out through the main door and on to the terrace. Then I blinked at what I saw.

There was a flicker of torches—and I mean the medieval kind with six-inch-long flames. Out on the lawn there was a milling crowd of people, not babbling like earlier, but gathered quietly in the torchlight. I was one of the last few stragglers, late again. I looked round the faces, still but shifting with the flicker, but Swan had been swallowed in among them. There was Albie, there was Maisie, only half familiar, with a glint of fire in their eyes.

There was Hob, beside me. 'Hey,' I said, 'what's happening?'

Usually he'd have a smile for me or a joke, but now he barely turned his head. He said, 'Look.'

Laura-Lee stood up on the edge of the terrace. No one was in charge, I knew, but if there was anything to organize, anything that needed a hot-line between us and Antonin or Dom, people would always look her way.

'OK,' she said, and everyone grew quiet. 'We all know what's happened. We're all cut up about it. But . . . ' She let the murmurs die down. 'But we're going to be practical.' She paused. 'If there are ever any questions— anyone from the outside—this is what happened. He walked out, last Thursday. We all heard him saying he was homesick. Saying he missed his girlfriend. Emma, he said. Then he packed his bags and went. End of story.' She looked around. 'Is that clear?'

'You mean . . . ' somebody piped up. 'You mean the police, that sort of thing?' It was a guy's voice, and it sounded nervous.

'There's no reason why it should come to that,' said Laura-Lee. 'No reason at all. But just in case . . . Nobody here wants people snooping, do we?' There was a shuffling of agreement. 'Right. Then let's make sure it stays that way.'

I looked at Hob. 'Is that why they've closed the front gate?'

He looked at me, inscrutable. 'The gate's always closed,' he said. 'I mean, Dom's collection upstairs . . . It's worth millions. People can't just walk in, stands to reason.'

'I thought we could just walk out.'

'We can. You just ask at the hut. The guy opens the gates.' Hob frowned a little. 'Didn't he let you?' That's when I felt stupid.

'Never mind,' I said. 'I didn't ask.'

At the edge of the crowd, something was happening. The torches were forming up in twos; they started moving, slowly, and all of us were falling into lines behind them. No one had given the orders, but we were moving down towards the gardens, a dark crocodile of us with torches at intervals, in pairs, like eyes. Every now and then a clutch of fresh torches would be passed back and someone new

135

would take one, reaching up to light it from a burning torch nearby. I had one in my hand—I hardly knew how it had got there—and someone had stopped to offer me their flame.

It was Ange. I'd never felt inclined to like her much, even before our talk in the kitchen earlier, when she was snide about Swan. But that was in the ordinary light of day. What is it about firelight, and darkness? Now she held her torch towards me, and I reached out mine, so the ends of them gently touched and quivered. For a minute nothing happened: hers burned, mine didn't. Then with a crackle and a spit of sparks mine took the flame, and we both looked up and smiled, like old friends. It could have been her, I thought, they'd wheeled in on the barrow; it could have been Albie, or Maisie, or any of the other names I hadn't learned yet. We were all in this together. We weren't that different, after all.

Where did it come from, that feeling? Twenty minutes earlier I'd been crouched in the bushes, planning a dash to the gate. Now here we were, shoulder to shoulder. It must have been the firelight, and the adrenalin, and the kind of whoosh you get when you've been tense and tired for weeks and weeks. Like working for exams . . . and then they're over. I felt sort of drunk, although I hadn't touched a drop since the initiation night. It was over now, surely, all that rivalry, all the whispering backbiting stuff. This awful thing had to happen to shake us, but now . . . And Swan was OK.

Down near the front, someone had started humming, a sort of lilting chant, and it spread back through the line as we walked. As we moved through the gardens, torchlight flickered on the statue faces; they were really stone, and really still, but the shifts of the light made them seem to turn and gravely look down on us, with their deep-bored eyes, as we went by. As we ducked through

136

the archway from the lowest garden, the line had to break and re-form, and it was a while before I realized that the walker at my side was Swan.

'Swan! Thank God you're OK.'

The words just came out, and I expected her to snap at me or turn away. She didn't. There was a kind of calm look in her eyes I hadn't seen before. 'What do you mean?'

'I thought . . . I mean, when I didn't see you . . . ' I trailed off. It felt silly now. I didn't want to say the kind of things we'd agreed not to, or she'd back off. She seemed relaxed and easy, softened by the firelight . . . and I wanted it to stay that way.

'I'm fine,' she said. 'I'm getting somewhere, Nick. Everything's going to work out. You've no idea . . . ' She was looking at me now, but as if she was looking faraway, beyond me. 'I'll tell you later.' Then, suddenly, she touched my hand. 'Take care,' she said softly. 'When they said you'd gone out after Matty . . . I was worried.'

'I was worried about *you*.' It was just a second, but she brushed her hand against mine. We walked on side by side.

We were further down into the grounds than I'd been yet. We were by the lakeside, passing the low wooden boathouse, which sloped from the bank into a little creek. We came out on to the promontory. Up above the lawns behind us, the big house blazed with lights in all its windows, and light spilled from its open doors.

Antonin was waiting at the folly. As the torches slowly gathered, the Doric columns stood out tall in the red glow of a little fire. Deeper back in the shadows was the wheelbarrow. Laid out along a low stone bench was something in a sheet, which must be Matty's body. I was glad of the sheet. I remembered those spikes. I'd imagined enough; I didn't want to see.

A silence settled round us. As we gathered round him, Antonin seemed to grow a little taller, and he spoke.

'We are here,' he said, 'to celebrate. Our friend Mattheus was a brave man. An explorer. He went further into the Work than most of us would dare. To that, we drink!' As he raised his glass there was a ripple round me. People were passing back cheap plastic cups and in them was a warm dark liquid with the smell of spice and wine. Antonin waited till we were still.

'Do not insult him,' he said, 'with the thought that he failed. That his work was wasted. No, think that maybe now he knows the secret.' He held his glass high. 'He has truly gone for stone. My friends . . . To Matty the Pan!'

He looked sideways, and there at the edge of the torchlight was one of the groundsmen with his spade in hand. At his side was a mound of cut turfs, and a narrow pit. I turned to Swan. 'Hey, they can't do that, can they?' Antonin nodded at the groundsman, who picked up Matty's body like a roll of carpet.

'My friends . . . ' said Antonin. 'To Matty the Pan!'

'To Matty the Pan!' And before the toasts were over, the body was slipped in the hole.

'They aren't allowed,' I said. 'It isn't legal.'

'Why not?' Swan whispered. 'It's what he'd have wanted. Where would they send him back to anyway?' She touched my arm again. 'He wouldn't be here, would he, if he had a family? Like all of us.'

For a flicker I saw Mum, and Malcolm, and my old house, like a cartoon couple in a young kid's picture book. Unreal. I'd been going to say 'Not like me,' but I couldn't. They looked the way Dad had looked in last night's dream—sad, slightly see-through. More real than that, there was Swan's hand resting on my forearm, light but warm.

Around us, the people were moving and talking again.

138

Swan raised her glass of punch; I raised mine, and as the chop of the spade and the dull sound of earth in the hole began I downed the punch in three quick glugs. It went down like sweet fire.

'Listen, Swan . . . ' I didn't know how to say it right. 'I . . . I don't know if I'd be here at all, if it wasn't for you.'

She looked down at the ground and bit her lip. I was losing her. But I mustn't stop now. 'I mean,' I went on, 'I've seen you working. You . . . you're good. I mean, you really can dance. You could be a proper ballerina.'

She gave a quick shrug. 'Five years too late,' she said. 'I grew. At least two inches too tall. So that was that.'

'It can't be.' I took a breath. 'I mean, you're beautiful.'

'Oh, Nick,' she sighed. 'Spare me. Beautiful? What does that mean? So blokes stare at me. Big deal.' She looked up, not angry now, just sad. 'So I do the statues. I could think of worse ways I could sell *beautiful*. Can't you?'

'Swan,' I said, 'I was frightened for you. Ange said you'd gone with Dom.'

'Ange! Angelic, isn't she?'

'She's jealous. She says the others are, too. What's going on?'

'What's going on,' she said, 'is I know I've got one chance. Just one. And the others know it too. Dom's choosy. He can afford to be. He's got the world to pick from. And if he doesn't want us, what's the point of all this? Well?'

'I don't care about Dom,' I said. 'I'm fed up with this endless Dom this, Dom that—in that creepy tone of voice, like they're talking in church.'

'Stop,' she said. 'I know how they talk about him—just because he's rich and all that. They don't *know* him.'

139

Suddenly the heat of the punch had worn off. 'Oh, yes?' I said. 'And you do?'

'A bit.'

'So it's true. You *were* Picked? You said . . . '

'No, I didn't. Look, I did my routine for him. We talked a bit.'

'Just talked?' I could hear my voice rising. 'From what I hear . . . '

'Don't believe anything you hear. Dom isn't like Antonin. He's not part of . . . all this.'

'What is he, then? What's in it for him?'

'He's a businessman. Really educated, too. A real expert. Anyway, you'll see.'

'Not very likely. Can't see me being Picked.'

'You don't know,' she said. 'I've told him about you.'

'You've what?'

She took a step back. The soft look had gone from her eyes. She was watchful again. 'Cool it, OK? We're friends, all right? If we're really careful—I mean, keep it professional—there's a chance that we can work together. Understand? But Nick, you mustn't get . . . too *involved*.'

'I'm not,' I said. 'I'm . . . ' But the words trailed off. If I wasn't *involved*, what was I?

'Anyway,' she said, 'you'll meet him. That's him over there.'

16

I looked towards Dom, and things went all slow-motion, like some cheesy moment in a film where two love-at-first-sighters spot each other in a crowded room. No, that's not what I mean. I mean it was like the moment in a car crash, when they say you see everything—pedestrians turning to stare, very slowly, and maybe a dog in mid-bark—in the long, weirdly calm moment just before the smash.

I can't say what I felt. All I knew was that there'd been days of watching and of being watched; there'd been my panic by the shut gate, then the rush of relief, and then the strange conviction that all these people were my true friends; there'd been the touch of Swan's hand, and the quiver when she said *I've seen Dom*. As if all that had been gathering into a storm cloud, and now it would burst.

I can't even say that I saw him, at first. I saw the others clustered round by the Folly. I knew by the way they were elbowing in, like moths to a candle, and yet trying to look casual, that the centre of the huddle must be him. He was watching me too, I knew it. He'd have seen me talking to Swan; he'd seen her touch me. How much more had he seen, these last days, as he watched us all, from upstairs windows, from peep-hole cameras? Suddenly I didn't care. Now Dom would have to meet me face to face.

The group parted slightly, and I saw him for the first time. The rest must have seen him lose interest in them, and turned one by one to look where he was looking. I

141

was walking towards him already. He was raising a hand, very slightly, and the path between us cleared.

There he was—our host, or should I say our landlord, or our owner? I'd like to say that he looked something special, or was flanked by huge bodyguards, but it was subtler than that. He was a middle-aged man, middle height, with trim grey hair and little glasses, dressed in a way you'd hardly notice—a jacket, I think, and a roll-neck—the kind of style that signals Casual But The Best.

Just a lift of the hand, and people cleared a path between us. There was something almost lazy in the way he looked. No need for theatricals—he had all it takes, the absolute assurance that big money brings. For all he knew I was going to rush at him, grab him by the throat and scream *Murderer!* I didn't, though I'm not sure why not, and he stepped towards me, holding out his hand.

'Amadeus. Swan has told me all about you.' The voice was quiet, cultured. If my dad had been there he'd have said it told the world that he'd been to a Good School, as surely as wearing an old school tie. He didn't need to speak up. There was silence round him, all the faces leaning inwards in the torchlight, hanging on his words. They looked from him, to me and Swan, to him, and back to me.

What was I meant to say?

Dom's eyes were as mild as Antonin's were fierce, but they held me. He was a collector after all—a connoisseur. I felt my skin tense, as if I were standing naked in front of them all. If I could break that gaze, I could think of some clever reply. But Dom didn't blink.

All I could do was hold out a hand, like a kid brought to meet some long lost uncle. Dom looked at my hand and smiled faintly. Then he took it—the ghost of a handshake, like a deal already clinched. I whisked my hand away.

142

'So sad about Matty the Pan,' he said. 'A waste. He was gifted.' Now Antonin was there, at the back; his look was fierce, not fawning like the rest.

'Ach!' said Antonin. 'Too much ego, and a little gift. Those things together . . . deadly.'

'You are a hard taskmaster,' Dom said, mildly.

'I have experience, that is all,' said Antonin. 'If you listened to me . . . I say the Pan was not ready.'

Dom did not look at him. 'Who can tell why people do these things?' he said to everybody. Everybody nodded as if they agreed. 'Who can tell?' Dom said again, and looked straight at me.

'Pretty obvious.' That was me. The words had slipped out. There was an indrawn breath around me. Swan was staring like the others. Dom had me in that pale gaze again. There was no way I could back out now.

'Oh?' said Dom.

'I mean . . . he was totally gutted. Everything he'd worked for . . . All he wanted was . . . ' How could I say what he'd wanted? Dom must know.

'Poor boy,' Dom said. 'Really?' He looked so innocent, so butter-wouldn't-melt . . . I flared.

'You picked him up . . . and dropped him.' There was a *Ssssh!* around me. 'What did you expect?'

'We have to be realistic.' Dom's voice was level. 'Everyone knows when they come here: I can only use the best.'

'What gives you the right . . . ?' I think I was shouting.

'Nick!' It was Swan's voice behind me—and my real name, too. Dom had lifted his hand again, in that gesture that stopped her in mid breath.

'It's true,' said Dom. 'No right. There are no rights in the real world, believe me. But there are things I can do, and people seem to want them.'

143

'In exchange for what?'

Dom smiled. 'I like your spirit,' he said. 'Like your friend Swan. She has spirit. I can work with that.'

'Raw!' It was Antonin. 'He's raw. Not ready. No technique.'

'Thank you, Antonin,' Dom said, still looking at me. In the hush, the groundsman's spade went softly on. 'We must talk more,' Dom said. I couldn't speak. I didn't need to. There was something in that never-blinking gaze that told me he saw everything that flickered through my head. You could almost want to trust him.

As if he'd seen that thought too, he smiled. 'When you feel ready,' he said, 'you must come and visit me.'

Behind us, the groundsman's digging had come to a stop. I heard him patting the earth down with the flat of the spade. Dom had gone. We were emptying back past the boathouse. In the little groups around me there was a simmer of whispers I couldn't catch. I could guess, though. Dom had spoken to me. They'd all have noticed.

No way was I going to see him. Was that what it meant, to be Picked? But it wasn't an order. *When you feel ready,* he'd said. I remembered that voice, and that touch. My skin crept.

When I felt ready. That would never be.

'OK, OK!' Laura-Lee clapped her hands. 'This hasn't been a party. We've got work tomorrow.'

'Shall we do some work now?' It was Maisie's voice, like a child's, wheedling. 'I feel I could really . . .'

'Indeed,' Antonin cut in. 'A significant moment. I shall supervise.'

The torches went out one by one. As we trooped back through the lower garden, I realized that Swan was still beside me. Neither of us had spoken, but she hadn't

144

slipped away. After all this time watching for her, waiting, we should have been talking, but . . . There was a kind of dull fog in my mind.

What was I doing here? I didn't understand. I'd been within sight of the world outside the gate, and missed my chance. No, I'd chosen to stay. I'd come back for Swan, that's what I told myself but was that all? Five minutes back inside and I was marching with the rest of them. I remembered the moment with the torches, where I'd lit mine from Ange's. That wasn't friendship; that was bonding; that was being in a tribe. Was I fooling myself with these thoughts of escape? Maybe I just couldn't imagine life in the real world any more?

'What are you thinking?' Swan said.

'Nothing.' I looked at her. In the moonlight, she was looking at me in a way I couldn't make out.

'Be careful,' she said.

'Sorry. Have I blown it?'

'No. He liked you.' She gave a faint smile. 'Can't think why.'

'Me neither.' Then we were quiet again. I was tired, just tired. We walked up to the house together, almost touching, and she didn't move away.

'Goodnight then,' she said by the staircase. 'See you.' She touched her lips to my cheek. Then she was gone, up the stairs to the women's room, and I was blinking as if I'd just been startled out of sleep. 'Swan?' I called after her. Had she really done that? But she didn't look back, and there was no reply.

It was several minutes before I moved. The last of them came straggling past me, most of them going upstairs. Somewhere, probably the long room, Antonin's extra work was starting. That was the last thing I could see myself doing. Or the next to last thing; suddenly, the least likely was sleep.

I paced. In a while, surely, my heart would stop its thudding. I went out on the terrace and paced up and down, while the lights went out upstairs. Then it was quiet, with just the all-night whisper of water. The culvert. I walked round the back of the building, making it last, breathing deeply. I needed cool air. I watched the moonlight shifting as clouds trailed past it, and the shifting shadows of the house, the wall, the statues, and the trees. I needed to stop my mind replaying every word I hadn't said to Swan. *Fool, fool,* I was thinking. Why hadn't I just said *I love you*? Back inside I found an alcove in the shadows of the hall. What if Swan had realized she couldn't sleep either? What if she came back down, for me?

I might have dozed a little, because the voice, when it came, seemed to be echoing from very far away.

'Trash! Garbage!' I made the words out gradually, and though the voice was muted I could hear it getting sharper, shriller, almost a laugh now, then almost a shriek. It was deep in the building, downstairs. It was Antonin. He was hurling insults; one moment he was taunting, teasing, needling someone as I'd seen before, the next he was over the top, out of control, in a rage. 'Filth! You bag of skin and piss!' I was up on my feet, and making for the long room. Why weren't doors thrown open all over the building, and everyone streaming out saying, *What's going on?* There was no one. But it was louder now; I was getting closer, close enough to hear his breath between the words, panting, then a dull thud, thud, and panting again.

Or was that another voice, gasping for breath? Was that a whimper, or a groan?

'Look!' Antonin's voice was clear now. 'Look, the idiot bleeds! I will not have it! Call yourself a statue? I will not tolerate bleeding!' And the same low thud, thud, thud again.

146

Then it had stopped. Somewhere, I thought I still heard ragged breathing, someone really hurt, but it could have been anywhere, nowhere, or still in my head. At the door of the long room I froze, listening. Nothing. Slowly I eased it open and looked in. It was dark and empty. I made for the gym.

I stopped by the gym door, tense. There was no sound, but the light was on. There they were, two or three of them, in their postures. They looked calmly into nowhere, straight ahead. Nobody moved as I peered in.

There was no sign of Antonin, or anybody hurt or weeping. Yet it must have been here, whatever had happened. It must have been right alongside them, but they'd been Working, and that's all that mattered, and they hadn't stirred.

17

I stood outside the gym door for a long time, stalled. What could I do? Who could I tell? What I'd heard—Antonin's jeers and cracked laugh and the sobbing afterwards—was bad enough. The worst thing was that it seemed to be normal. In the sane world, people would have been throwing open doors and windows, raising the alarm. Here, no one moved a muscle, literally. In the sane world, someone would have been phoning the police. I thought of last night, on the terrace. *Nobody here wants people snooping, do we?* said Laura-Lee. I remembered the mutter of agreement. *Let's make sure it stays that way.*

Anyway, there were no phones. I hadn't noticed that at first, but there were lots of things I hadn't noticed.

There was a sound in the gym, and the practice was ending; I heard footsteps coming, and I shifted. I slipped into the bedroom just before the people who'd been Working, so anyone else would have guessed that I'd been in the gym with them. It wasn't a good time to look like an outsider. *He's too fond of skulking in corners by himself*—I remembered the edge in Ange's voice when she mentioned Hob. *Look out for yourself. Be careful*, Hob said. Until now I'd never quite seen why.

I lay in bed and tried to sleep.

Swan. It hadn't been Swan, had it? The voice I heard crying, it didn't sound like hers. Then again, I hadn't heard her crying. No, I'd seen her go upstairs. But what if she'd crept down again, when I wasn't looking? What if . . . ?

148

No! I had to stop this. My mouth was dry, my heart was thudding. I mustn't think these things. I was getting obsessed, like everybody else here. I must try not to think. That's when I started imagining creeping down the women's corridor to find Swan, just to make sure . . .

. . . and somewhere down that corridor I slipped asleep, because I found a door that wasn't there, a door I knew, and opened it. There was my room, in my old house, but there was no space for me in it, because Albie's automaton was lying in my bed. I could hear Mum and Malcolm in the kitchen, making breakfast, all quite normal. How come they hadn't noticed the thing in the bed wasn't me? I went into the kitchen to tell them, but it wasn't them: it was the Stone Saints. Things were a mess; the toast was burning, and I wanted to tell them that this is how it starts, giving up, like Dad had, letting things get out of hand. They would never be much good at anything and their break in life would never come. Then one of them leaned over to the other, ignoring the smoking toaster, and it was that moment I'd first seen them—one reaching very gently to wipe the other's eye, like a mother and child or a husband and wife the way it's meant to be. And for some reason I found myself crying in the dream.

I woke with the day's usual clatter. Everyone else was throwing clothes on, going down to breakfast, as if it was just any other day.

The dining room was nearly full. No Swan yet. She would be down in a minute, and I would know I'd been stupid to be scared last night. For now, the packets of cereal reassured me. With their silly bright colours and cartoons and amazing free offers of things not even a kid of five would want, they were the real world, still going on somewhere without me. All over the Western world

149

ordinary families were sitting down, grumpy, rushed, and hassled, to packets like these. My old friends would be sitting down to breakfast. Mum and Malcolm would be sitting down to breakfast too. Even that was a sort of a comfort. There was still a real world.

But the voice in the night . . . That had been real too. Antonin, and the sobbing, and the thud of flesh and bone.

'Wasn't it wonderful?' Ange sat beside me.

'What?'

'By the lake. So moving.'

I tried to make the right noise. I had to talk to someone, but it wasn't her. 'Uh . . . where are the others? Sleeping in?'

She glanced at me. 'No. Except for you-know-who, of course.' I had a cold feeling all over. You know *who*? I glanced round. Swan was still not there. 'Little Miss Perfect!' Ange said. 'Got what she was asking for.'

I had to wait a moment, so it wouldn't be too obvious. I'd stopped breathing. Count to ten, very slowly. Then I pushed my plate aside. I think I muttered something about toast.

I knocked on the women's room door. I'd never been down that corridor; I'd just kind of accepted, like I'd accepted so much else, that it was out of bounds. Now, I could feel my skin prickling at the thought I might be caught, though what would happen if I was I didn't know.

No reply. I held my breath. There was a slight sound, the creak of a bed. 'Swan!' I whispered. No answer, except maybe a sigh, almost a groan. I went in.

Inside, it was still half dark. On one bed a bundle of bedclothes shifted; half a face looked out. I knew at a

150

glance that the dark patch round the one eye wasn't shadow. She heaved over and groaned; the sheet slipped back.

It wasn't Swan.

Maisie was in her statue costume, though the skirt looked rucked and torn. She eased herself up on one elbow. 'What . . . ?' I started.

'I fell down, OK?'

'It was Antonin, wasn't it? I heard him. I tried to find what was happening but . . . ' My eyes were getting used to the half light, and I tailed off as I saw her face. It was a mess of bruises. 'I mean, I never guessed . . . '

She shrugged. 'It's not your business.'

'Not my business? Somebody should *stop* him. I mean, he's really flipped now, hasn't he? You've got to tell somebody. Tell Dom. He's the boss round here.'

'No!' It was such a sharp sound, almost a wince, that I thought it was physical pain. 'No, don't,' she said more quietly. 'Look, Antonin's got . . . very high standards, that's all.'

I had a queasy feeling in my stomach. He had done this to her. Was I hearing this right: she was defending him?

'Look,' she said urgently, 'I wasn't trying hard enough. I thought I was being clever, showing off. Sometimes he needs to put us in our place. It's for our own good.'

'That's as mad as he is. We've got to tell Dom.'

'No!' The fierceness of it stopped me. She was trembling, eyes bright in their purple bruises. 'Oh my God, does it show?' She scrabbled for her make-up mirror and stared at herself. I heard her gasp.

'There,' I said. 'Tell Dom.'

'No!' she almost shouted. 'You really don't understand, do you? Dom's a collector. Do you think he'll even *look* at spoiled goods?' She stared in the mirror again, and tried to smooth her hair down to hide the bruises. 'You say a word about this,' she said, 'and I'll tell them it was you who did it. Understand?' She held me in her gaze until I nodded. 'Right,' she said, quietly now. 'Have you thought what it's like, to be thrown out? Don't you understand? Of course Matty wanted to die.'

She reached up to the window, pulled the curtain open a crack, and flinched at the light.

'What's going on here, Maisie?' I said. 'It's like one of those cults. They've brainwashed you.'

'What do you know about it? I've seen weird groups— Moonies, Jesus Army . . . Plenty of us have—when you're on the edge they come swarming round—they seem to smell it. Parents always say their kids were brainwashed; they just made up their minds differently, that's all. I was in one place, they did a lot of chanting. It felt good. I guess I got myself a bit spaced out, what with all that and no sleep. The people panicked, had me whisked off to the local loony bin. That's when I saw through them: all their talk about enlightenment and that stuff. They weren't *serious*. My problem wasn't that I'd done too much; I hadn't done *enough*.' She sounded calm now, sort of logical. 'I was just out of hospital when I met Laura-Lee. She was on a recruiting run with Antonin. When I heard him talk, I realized: that's what I'm after. He's got this . . . vision. All about the place where life and the other thing meet.'

'You mean death,' I said.

'No. I mean not-life. Stone. Being dead is what life does. I mean . . . lasting for ever. Once you've felt it, nothing else will do.'

'Like Matty?' I said, as calm as I could manage.

'Matty? He wasn't ready for it. He thought it was just about . . . success. He hadn't even started on the deeper meaning. He wasn't prepared.'

Then she had me by my sweatshirt, clenching it till it

nearly tore. 'That's why we need Antonin, don't you see? You get the call from Dom and you're not ready, you end up like Matty. Once you get that far, there's no way back.'

'That far? What do you mean? How do you know?'

Her grip relaxed, but she leaned closer. 'Don't tell the others,' she said. 'But he gave me just a tiny glimpse.' Her eyes had a strange bright look, not quite natural, like fluorescent light. 'One day, when I'm really ready,' she said in a whisper, 'one day . . .'

There was more, but I'd stopped listening. She wasn't looking at me, but somewhere else beyond me. I thought of last night: it might have been the torchlight and the dark, but . . . hadn't someone looked at me like that?

Swan . . . This place was starting to get inside her, the way it had got Maisie. Swan was in danger. I had to find her, now.

Downstairs, the dining room was empty. They were gathering on the terrace for a session, but Swan wasn't there. She wasn't in the gym or in the Cool Room either. As I rushed from room to room I realized: Swan had disappeared again.

When you weren't looking for Hob he'd appear from nowhere, in the corner of your eye. Now when I wanted him he was nowhere to be found. I had to talk to someone half sane. *Skulking in corners,* Ange had said. I wish I knew what corner he was skulking in now.

I crept up to a window and peered through the bunched-up curtains. There were the others, on the terrace. And there was Antonin. I felt my teeth grit as I saw him, calm and smiling, moving from one person to the next, observing and advising. He looked like a man who'd had a good night's sleep, with nothing on his mind. But Hob wasn't there.

We had a cat once, at home, and it taught me a lot about cats' instincts. Given a choice, it would always climb up on a chair, a sideboard even, and look down. So it could pounce before it was pounced on, I guess. There was something in the way Hob tended to appear on walls that made me think of that.

I was up in the men's room in a few bounds, looking out. Careful . . . Even from that height, if I stared at Antonin's back, I had a feeling that he'd know. Now, very, very carefully, I eased open the window, stopping at the first hint of a creak and ducking down, then getting up very, very slowly and easing again.

Hob was there, on the little ledge outside the window. He was Working, statue-still. At any other time, it would have been a good game: I eased myself out and I was on the ledge behind him. In another life, I might have said Boo! As it was, I reached out a hand, very carefully, and touched him on the shoulder. He startled, so hard that for a moment I thought Antonin would swivel round and see. But Hob had discipline. He didn't turn his head.

'Amadeus?' he whispered.

'Come inside,' I said. 'I've got to talk to you.'

'Can't. Antonin will notice.'

'Tell him you needed a pee break,' I hissed. 'Just one minute. It's urgent.' Without answering, he started to move back in a flowing sort of crouch towards the window—so smoothly that Antonin passed right below us and didn't look up.

'Now, what's up?' Hob said when we both got inside.

'What's up? I've stopped pretending, that's all. Stopped pretending this isn't a madhouse. I mean, Antonin . . . What kind of nutter is he?'

'You said *one minute*,' Hob said, with a kind of smile.

'Help me. Can I trust you?' He nodded, very slightly. 'Tell me where she's gone,' I said.

'Who?'

'Swan. Come on, don't tell me you don't know. You're the star watcher round here.'

He glanced around, then leaned closer. 'I thought you knew,' he said. 'Everyone knows. She's up with Dom.'

For the second time that day the floor seemed to lurch beneath me. Dom . . . The thing that really chilled me about Maisie wasn't when she talked about Antonin—it was the weird light in her eyes when she mentioned Dom. *He gave me a glimpse*, she'd said, and that was what had trapped her in all this. *One day, one day* . . .

'Up where?' I said.

'Cool it. Look, I know you've got a thing for her, but . . . You've got to fend for yourself in this place. She will, that's for sure.'

'*Where?*'

'In the Apartment.'

'Where's that?'

'Where Dom lives.' I must have been looking dense. I'd been all around the upstairs of the house. I hadn't seen him there. 'It's, like, the attic,' he said. And I thought of the tall blank windows I'd seen from the sculpture garden, watching, watching.

'You've been there,' I said.

'No way. It's dead private. You only go if you're Picked.'

'You've never been?'

He gave a little grin. That's when I knew that I could trust him. 'Come off it,' he said, 'I'm not crazy. If the others are keen, I just say *After you* . . . '

'How do I get there?'

'Can't be done. There's only one door. The rest are locked. He's always got a guy on duty.' I must have looked

155

puzzled again. 'Come on, you didn't think all those groundsmen were just trimming the lawns.'

'Where's the door?' I said.

He had a weary sort of look as he told me. 'Thanks,' I said. 'You're a mate. Any other advice?'

'Yes,' he said. 'Don't. Just let her go.'

It was the mention of the groundsmen got me thinking. I wasn't a burglar by nature, but I'd need some tools. I waited till the rest streamed in to Antonin's next session, then I slipped away. The workshop door was ajar. Inside, there came the steady rasp of steel on stone.

I flattened myself against the doorpost and peered through the crack. He was head down, hunched over a bench at the back, his shoulders going with a steady motion. Parts of broken statues lay around, a head, a hand with missing fingers, and there were the tools, long saws and rasps and chisels. Blades for lighter work, too, sharp and thin and glinting, and tweezers and probes. A clutter of body-parts in wood or wax or plastic. There was an opened-up torso with its wicker rib-cage showing, waiting to be dismantled or repaired. By a metal sink on the far wall was a tray of little clamps and scalpels that made me think of the dentist's surgery, and wince.

On a trestle nearer to the door there was a scatter of the kind of tools I might have found in the garage at home. As I stepped into the room I kept an eye on the stonemason. He did not budge, still working with that steady motion, and I saw he had a stone bust laid out on the bench and he was working on the head. The face. He had a slow drill, making boreholes in its eyes.

A claw-hammer, a screwdriver, a chisel . . . This was no time to be fussy. I was out of the workshop in less than a minute and looking around me, all my senses going like a hunted animal. If anyone caught me now, with the tools in my hand, no way could I explain myself. The house was still, with everyone at work. There'd never be a better chance. I glanced up the back of the building . . . to the narrow gabled window, jutting up into the roof, that must be Dom's apartment. He had Swan. I thought of Maisie's bruised face, and Matty the Pan in the wheelbarrow, dripping. Whatever it was Dom did to them—the *lucky* ones, the ones who got Picked—he'd be doing it to her. I couldn't guess what it was. I only knew: she needed me. Quite what I'd do when I found her . . . I'd have to find out. For now, I'd started. No turning back. Just go.

18

The door was on the landing, not straight ahead but to one side, almost hidden by a huge grandfather clock. If I'd noticed it at all, I'd have thought it was a cupboard. So. The house was Dominic's, and everything outside as far as the eye could see . . . but he lived in it undercover, like the secret attic where Anne Frank hid in the Second World War. What had he got to hide from . . . or to hide?

I shrank back in the corner, clutching my tool kit. I had to move fast, but I also had to think.

Don't go through that door, Hob had warned me: there'd be a man on duty. Bodyguards inside, and that locked gate outside, operated by remote control . . . All this had been going on, as invisible as Dom himself, upstairs while we were having our little rivalries, playing our drama games and dressing up like kids. It had all seemed such important business, down there: after all, weren't we a commune, weren't we artists, weren't we . . . ?

Blink, and look again. Dom's was the real business. He was the collector. Every now and then he reached downstairs and plucked one of us. What was this whole place but a human statue nursery?

I had to think. If Hob was right and there was *always* a man on duty, it couldn't always be the same man. They must work shifts. And if they went on and off duty, how come I'd never seen one in the house?

There was a back way in, there had to be. When people

158

built a house like this, there'd have been servants. For a moment I could almost hear Dad's voice—those days he seemed to take us to some stately home so he could give a gloomy little speech about it. The class system. *Don't be so negative,* Mum would say again. He'd been a Communist, before he met Mum. Once she turned to me and said, 'Your father's a dinosaur.' That was before they'd split up and I thought, at the time, it was a joke. Afterwards, I wasn't so sure.

'Dozens of servants,' Dad's voice muttered. 'The big folk wouldn't have wanted guests to see them cluttering up the place. There'd have been the back stairs for the likes of them.'

That meant the back of the house. I was going to have to go back down, outside, and start again. I'd have to cross the courtyard, and . . . I thought again. That first night, Maisie had led us out under the house—a kind of tunnel—right from the stable yard where the van had pulled in. If there was a back way, that was where it would be.

I crept out on the terrace, and the place had never felt so tense and still, or the gravel so loud underfoot. I kept close against the wall, round to the steps down. In the damp dark of the cellars, I could breathe again.

There must be a staircase. This far under the house, it was dark as evening, but I felt my way. On my right was the door we'd come through, I was almost sure. Faintly, that way, I heard voices. It was the Cool Room up there, not far away, where we all lounged together, chatting and unwinding, watching TV. For a second I felt a twinge: why couldn't I be up there with the others, and there be a simple explanation for all this, and we'd have a good laugh about it after, or better still none of it had ever happened at all?

But Swan . . . I had to find her. In the dark I felt my

159

way along the other wall. And yes, there it was, a doorway, made of metal, and flush to the wall. It was locked. I felt and found the keyhole: a Yale. I didn't stop to think, but I had the screwdriver out and rammed the point down in the crack, to lever the catch out from behind. I hadn't even known I knew how to . . . but in a crisis it's surprising what you do.

Inside, the stairs were dark, still with the basement feeling. There was only one way to go: up. I'd done it now—breaking and entering—and if anyone caught me there was no way I could say I was just passing by. All I could do was move fast. Swan was up there somewhere, and if I could get in this way, I could bring her out.

The stairs turned once, and there was light above me. Suddenly my flesh was prickling, because there was another sound. As I crept up to the little landing I made it out more clearly: it was the tinny patter of a radio, doing the sports news, and it came from a room with its door ajar, on my left. I froze. On my right was an outside door, that must lead out into the courtyard. That one was bristling with serious locks; no way would I have got in through there with my screwdriver. Straight ahead were more stairs leading up.

I eased my weight up the last step, on to the landing. The door to the room on my left was open just enough for me to see a table, and a mug of coffee. Then someone moved; I heard a chair creak, out of sight behind the door, and the radio got louder. The football results! I muttered a prayer of thanks to whichever team he supported, and I made my move.

I was round the turn of the upper stairs before I paused again. I was into Dom's domain now, I could feel it. It may have been a different paint, or carpet, but I could smell it in the air. The smell of wealth, Dad would have said. Nothing obvious—that would be tasteless, *nouveau riche*. With real wealth you can't see quite what it is, but you know.

At the top of the stairs was one more door. Not locked, this time. When I opened it, I'd be in the inner sanctum. No going back then. I tried the handle, carefully; it turned. OK, let's go.

It was the size of the place that hit me. That and the stillness of it, so I held my breath, the way you do in a church. The windows were high and narrow and the light cut in at an angle, hardly touching the rest of the gloom.

I know about attics. We had one at home. You climbed up a ladder, through a little hatch, then you scrambled in on hands and knees. It was heaped up with cardboard boxes and old carpets. When you came down your skin itched all over from that insulating stuff they put between the beams.

This wasn't so much an attic as a warehouse. The whole top of the house had been opened up, right to the roof, and there was a great brass chandelier—glinting now in the half-light, not lit. Yes, the place had a churchy feel, with dust specks rising in the shafts of sunlight. I couldn't imagine *speaking* in the quiet of it, like a library. No, not a library—a museum. All round were statues, some shrouded in dustsheets, some on plinths, some propped up or lying still half-packed in wooden cases. So this was Dom's collection. If I'd thought the few sculptures in the garden or the house were it, I'd been massively wrong.

I stepped out from the doorway cat-foot, ready to duck and run. But it was quiet and still—no voices, not a trace of people. It felt like a building locked up for the night. I felt ridiculous, standing there with my amateur housebreaker's kit in my hand. I laid the tools down, quietly, and walked among the clutter of stuff in a kind of a daze.

On one side, the wide painted face of an ancient Egyptian sarcophagus stared out at me, with a blank smile on its fleshy painted lips. Next to it was a smaller casket, this time in metal, but still with the same features, smaller, smaller . . . then something like the pupa of a large insect, only it had come unswaddled at the top. and I saw it was human—the mummy itself, painstakingly unpeeled, with the papery skin tight to the forehead and the lips pulled back from long uneven teeth. It was hardly a person, this thing like a shrivelled curled up leaf. And yet it had been. I didn't know which was more awful: to be stopped on the journey to the next life, stuck as a museum exhibit, or to arrive in the next world as shrunken and shrivelled as this.

Ghastly, to buy and sell things like this. It felt wrong, and was it even legal? Or were these the things Dom couldn't display in his expensive London gallery? For the first time it struck me that Dom, the connoisseur, the world-class dealer, might have his own reasons for keeping this place private, just as much as Antonin or any of us runaways.

But where was Swan?

I picked my way, in half-light, through the shapes. They all had faces and they looked at me, and as I walked past it was hard to look away. There were three or four terracotta soldiers from the famous Chinese tomb. Good copies, or no . . . Dom would be dealing in the real thing. With money like Dom seemed to have, he could arrange it, never mind the law and Customs. He'd have friends to help him do it, too.

There were Balinese puppets, flat shapes with long eyes and long smiles and impossibly thin dancing limbs. They were next to a waxwork, life size and lifelike apart from that too glossy look on its skin. That was no antique. Queasily, I recognized her, and her flawless toothy

162

smile—a children's TV show presenter from years and years ago. Then there was a Punch and Judy booth, a crash test dummy and a case of dolls, all mixed together—rag dolls, Barbies, and a crude wax thing with roughly painted features and some rusty pins in its heart and its stomach, for a witch's curse. There was a ventriloquist's dummy with its slack hinged jaw. Maybe all these things were stolen goods . . . or maybe they all catered for the same weird taste. All of them were almost human—almost but not quite—or like the mummy they'd been human once and had become a thing.

But Swan . . . Somewhere, somewhere nearby, she was with Dominic. I was wasting time, letting this stuff fascinate me. I didn't know how, but I just had to get her out of here.

I'd come halfway down the hall by now, and the light was changing. At the far end, a lamplight glow leaked out behind a screen. I wished I'd kept hold of the hammer, but I wasn't going back for it. I came round behind a glass case. Looking through it, past something Egyptian, the jackal-headed god, maybe, I would see where the light came from, and trust that anyone there would see their own reflection in the glass, not me.

Just for a moment, I was dazzled. There were bare bulbs, bulbs and their reflections in a mirror, and that mirror in another mirror, and . . . I couldn't tell which view of Swan, face-on, back, or profile, was the real one. It was a dressing room, like in a theatre, and she was putting careful touches to her make-up, in her ballerina gear.

And Dom? No sign of him. If he'd been there, would she have been so unselfconscious, with half her skin plaster white, half pink and bare? This was backstage. I could have felt embarrassed, once. Not now. This was the best thing I could have hoped for. I stepped out round the glass case, willing her *Don't be startled, don't call out* . . . 'Hey, it's me.'

For an instant she froze, the make-up poised, then whipped round. 'Nick! Have you talked to him?'

'Dom? No.'

'Then how . . . ? He didn't call for you?'

This was no time for explanations. 'Let's get out of here.'

Her scarlet lips went tight. 'What are you talking about?' she said. 'You'll spoil everything.'

Then I was angry. 'How can you?' I hissed. 'After what he did to Matty . . . ?' And her eyes flared too.

'What do you know about it? What *did* he do?'

'I . . . I don't know. But you saw him, you saw Matty, didn't you?' I was right beside her now, and she was glaring. I grabbed her hands, and saw her mouth open as if she might scream; I dropped her hands and they hung there, half stretched out towards me, as if she was offering me something in her arms.

Her arms. There was Ange's voice in my mind: *You've noticed her arms . . . ?* My eyes dropped to the place inside her elbows, and then slowly down to the wrist. It was the first time I'd seen her forearms bare, without make-up, and as if in slow motion, like a camera slowly tracking in to close-up, I knew what was written there for me to read. I don't know much about drugs, but I'd seen videos at school; I knew what kind of thing it had to be—the little puckered marks of healed-up scabs, the slightly swollen veins. More shocking, on Swan's left wrist, there were a couple of straight white scars, not just scratches, not accidental. I remembered what Ange had said. *She's desperate . . . She's been through Hell.* I must have stopped in mid breath, because Swan noticed me looking, and let me look a second longer, before folding her arms across her waist.

164

'Happy now?' she said, with no expression I could read. 'Satisfied?'

'I . . . didn't know.'

'Now you do. Have you changed your mind about me?' She was glaring at me with that fierce blank look but under it I saw her quivering. Whether that was rage or tears I couldn't tell.

'No, I haven't changed my mind. I love you.'

I'd said it. She flinched slightly. That was all. 'Well,' she said quietly. 'Then let's do what we've got to.'

'We've got to get out of here.'

'What?' she said. 'What are you talking about? This is it, Nick. We've nearly made it.' She bit her lip. 'This is what it's all about.'

I shook my head and for a moment neither of us moved. Then she'd turned back to the glass. She was painting the make-up on her arms, tight-faced, in a kind of frenzy. I could hear her breathing—short gulps, as if she was about to cry.

'Swan, Swan . . . what've you got yourself mixed up in?' She didn't answer, dabbing at the thick mascara round her eyes. 'What . . . ?'

'No time,' she said. 'He mustn't see . . . ' As she put the finishing touches to the make-up she relaxed.

'Sod him,' I said, half to myself. 'Has he . . . touched you?'

She whipped round from the mirror, and all her reflections turned to look behind me, away, or aside. 'For Christ's sake, Nick,' she said. 'Use your head. Be practical.' Then she softened. 'Oh . . . sorry. Look, he's an art dealer. All he wants is statues. It's just business to him. And besides . . . ' She leaned towards me. 'Why worry? It's a job. You think he's rich? He's got clients out there who are loaded, mega-loaded. Do this right, we'll never have to work again.'

165

There was a long pause. 'We?' I said.

'Oh yes. That's why I thought you'd seen him. He's set his mind on it. He wants it to be you and me.'

19

There were footsteps. I looked up. There was a doorway that led round the corner, into a back room. That's where the footsteps came from—and they were coming closer.

I had hold of Swan's hand. I pulled, but she struggled. 'Come on!' I said. 'Quick!' The footsteps were nearer. I gave a tug, and she lost her balance, staggering out into the room with me. 'Let go!' she hissed. 'Or I'll scream.'

That stopped me. 'Help me. Help *us*,' she said. 'Please. If you can't . . . get out.' She jerked her hand away.

'Not without you.'

The steps came round the corner, and I ducked back. 'He's ready to see you, miss. Come . . . ' The man's voice stopped in mid breath. It wasn't Dom. 'Hey, what's this?' He was looking straight at me through the glass cabinet; inside, the jackal-headed thing watched both of us, coolly, one sideways-facing Egyptian eye on each side of its head. His glance shot to Swan, and back to me.

I threw myself sideways, and ran. Not sensible, maybe, but it was all wrong. We could have been out of here minutes ago. Swan should have said *Thank God* and come with me. Now there was this man—one of the gardeners, I guessed, who weren't exactly gardeners. Dom would need experts to keep an eye on all this.

The man didn't follow. As I glanced back, his hand went to his belt. I froze, but what he pulled from the small black holster wasn't a gun. It was a walkie-talkie. Keeping his eyes on me, he muttered a few words into it. I was

167

backing away, then ducked among the plinths and crates and dustsheets, keeping to the shadows, skirting shafts of light. And there was the door . . .

Which opened. And the other guard stepped in.

I dropped to a crouch, behind something big. It was an arm-wrestling machine from some old seaside pier, in the shape of a strongman with a curly moustache and a leopard skin. His shoulders were wide, and I thanked his maker for the cover as I slowly raised my head and peered through the crook of his muscle-bulging arm, then between his claw-like fingers. The first man was out of sight. The second was older, very upright, like a butler, but he looked tough. I held my breath, till he stepped forward, into the room, away from the doorway. Now . . .

As I leaped, something snagged my sweatshirt. It only pulled me up a second but I staggered, and as I twisted round the arm-wrestler, damn him, rattled on his base. The sound was enough; both men heard. I tried to double back, stumbling into the plinth. With a creak the figure's one working arm hinged down, clunk, like a hug from a horrible uncle with a hearty red-cheeked grinning face.

Then the two of them had me. There was no violence, exactly, just that certain feeling that, whatever I was thinking of, I'd better not try. The older man looked me up and down. 'Cool it,' he said to the younger one. 'It's one of the kids downstairs.'

'He was with the girl,' said the other one. 'He's new, isn't he? How do we know where he's come from?'

'I know who he is.' The older one was nodding slowly. 'His lordship wants to see him. Oh, and bring the ballerina. She's involved in this too.'

Dom looked up from his computer screen, and for a moment his face had no expression I could place. Then he swivelled his high-backed leather chair to face us. He didn't get up, just leaned back with a dry appraising look. 'Breaking and entering . . . Well, well. An enterprising boy.' He looked at the men. 'Thank you,' he said. 'I hope you didn't make him feel unwelcome.' He fixed a cooler look on the older man. 'I'd like a report on how he got in, Jarvis. Go see to it.' Then he turned to me. 'Enterprising . . . but unnecessary. After all, I'd already invited you. All you had to do was knock.'

There were a couple of chairs. 'Thank you,' he said to the younger man, and he withdrew—though he'd be just outside the door, I felt sure of that.

'I'm so sorry if there was any unpleasantness,' said Dom. There was a softness in his voice which should have been soothing, like a doctor with his bedside manner. 'You have to realize that I have things of considerable value in there. We have to keep on our guard. However . . .' He smiled, for the first time. 'Now you're with us, we can talk.'

After the warehouse of the attic the back room felt private and small, but the flicker of several screens along the desk behind Dom made it clear that this was the brains of the place. On one, the fuzzy blue tints of closed-circuit TV gave a glimpse of the statue garden; on another, the terrace . . . In one corner of the room, inside the doors of a wooden hatch, was a just-opened crate on a wooden pallet; the packing inside had been peeled back to show a head, the smiling inscrutable face of a Buddha. On the wall above him, leather-bound books stacked neatly on the shelves—some with bindings so ancient-looking they might crumble at a touch.

He saw me looking. 'Are you a book man? I'd guess you are, in a small way. So few children really know how to *read* these days.' He stroked the spines with his gaze. 'There are a few items there you won't find in the British

169

Library. Or not any more.' He met my eyes with just the slightest twinkle, like a shared joke. I made my lips form a smile.

Dom had folded his fingers, not quite like a man at prayer, and paused. 'I do have taste,' Dom said. 'I know the Swan has been saying I'm only a businessman. But you shouldn't believe a ballerina. In my line of business it's the *taste* they pay for.' He smiled. He looked so casual, so at ease—but there was something in the preciseness of the way his fingertips touched . . . No, nothing was by accident. This whole place was just the way he'd planned it, right down to the tangle of wild clematis on the walls, which any smart gardener would have rooted out. It was deliberate, just as much as the slightly faded plum-red jacket with the silk scarf tucked in loosely at his neck. This was Dom's world. I'd thought it was Antonin's, but the words of the cliché dropped into my mind like a voice-over: *He who pays the piper calls the tune.*

'I won't ask you why you did it,' he said, letting his glance track to Swan and back at me. When Dom had chosen Antonin to be the guru of this place, he might have been going for the exact opposite of himself. One was bony, dark, and angular, the other comfortable, smooth, and trim. Antonin looked like an ascetic; Dom looked like a man with a taste for the fine things. Not greedy, though. He looked like a wine taster, who rolls the taste around his mouth then spits it out.

'Don't think I haven't noticed,' he said, in his bedside manner, 'that there's a certain . . . *electricity* between you.' I looked at Swan, but she was staring at the carpet. 'It's rather appealing—and *rare*, in a setting like this. We see plenty of little flings and flirtations, of course. The group ethos sorts that out, quite sharply. But most of the time they're at each other's throats. It is rare to find two young people who actually *care*.' He leaned back,

170

with a little sigh, and seemed to contemplate the ceiling. We waited.

'I assume this . . . episode was a rescue attempt?' He looked at me. 'Of course. But your friend here, she could have walked out any time she wanted. Isn't that so, my dear?' He waited, till she nodded.

'So you know that she's safe, and well, and happy. If that's all you wanted, you can leave.'

This was too much. 'I know what goes on in this place,' I said.

Dom raised his eyebrows. 'Oh?'

'I mean Antonin. I know what he does.'

'He is . . . highly strung. He is some kind of genius, after all.'

'He's mad. See what he did to Maisie.' For the first time there was a flicker of a question in Dom's eyes. 'He beat her up,' I said. 'I saw the bruises. She was black and blue.'

'*Did* he?' Dom's hands gripped the arms of his chair. His face didn't alter—still that pale almost-teasing slight smile—but his whole body stiffened. 'You mean,' he said, 'he damaged her? Left marks?' As if called, the younger man appeared in the doorway. 'Go and tell Monsieur Asch,' said Dom in a tight voice, 'that I wish to see him.'

'I have no use,' said Dom as he turned back, 'no use at all, for damaged goods. You must excuse me,' he said, suavely again, 'that is the businessman speaking. What I really want to talk about is you. Your . . . prospects. You are talented young people. You are learning the arts that Monsieur Asch can teach. And as I said, you have something else, between you, that is rare. The question is: are you prepared to use it?'

Swan broke the hush first. 'What . . . what do you want us to do?'

171

Almost gently, our host laughed. 'Don't worry—nothing that could possibly offend you. As I said, I have taste. No, I'm offering you a chance—the kind of chance your colleagues downstairs dream of. I believe that I might have a client, an important one, who would be interested in you.'

'You're, like, an agent?' I said. 'What's this—street theatre?'

'Alas, there is no money in the public arts. I deal with private clients. Many people collect statues, of course. A select few specialize in the human kind.'

So that was it. I wondered what Gloria had been doing in Mauritius, with all that swimming pool and sea. But we should try to sound professional. 'What are the terms?' I said.

'Good, I like a man who thinks practically.' Dom leaned forward. We were doing business. 'If you mean an Equity contract, well, this is a different world. But the rewards are in a different league, equally.' He paused. 'All expenses paid, of course. Sea, sun . . . Life in the kind of setting you only see in the Sunday supplements—the client I've got in mind owns a small Greek island, by the way. You'll become part of the household. Shopping trips to the finest shops in Athens. And the tips you get, if you do well . . . need I say more? Oh, and if you need a new name and a new ID—most of our young people seem to—that will be arranged. An attractive package, wouldn't you say?'

'And time off?'

'Time off? I'm describing most young people's perfect holiday! But you can leave any time you want to. You stay as long as you want to. And I can guarantee, believe me, that you'll want to stay. And all you have to do is use your talents—be the best double statue act ever. Hard work, but I believe you can. Don't you?'

172

I glanced at Swan. She looked Dom in the eye. 'Of course,' she said.

'Good, so we have a bargain? Yes?' This was addressed to me, and I felt Swan's eye on me too. *Help me. Help us.* I'd heard the desperation in it. She'd say yes, whatever I might say or do.

'A bargain,' I said.

'Then,' said Dom, 'let's drink to it.' From the drawer of his desk he drew a bottle—squat and dark, with an ornate label, like an expensive liqueur. He poured three little glasses.

I've never liked liqueurs much—makes me think of bad family Christmases—but I wasn't going to act like a kid now. 'To our business proposition!' As I knocked it back I gasped. It stung.

'This,' said Dom sniffing his glass, 'is a rare thing, too. Cloudberries. Only at their best within the Arctic Circle. Fortunately I have contacts in St Petersburg.' He watched Swan steadily, till she'd downed hers too.

'You two are . . .' Dom paused, savouring the next thought privately, 'almost an organism. If we can catch that in a statue act . . . I have a client in mind who has a rather old-fashioned and touching interest in a certain story. One of love, the tragic kind. Do you know the Greek myths? Orpheus and Eurydice . . .'

It might have been the unexpectedness of all this, or the drink, but his voice seemed to be coming from somewhere on the inside of my head. I looked up, and the room seemed very full of detail, and a bit too far away.

'She died,' he said, half to himself, 'from an unfortunate encounter with a snake. He went down to the underworld to save her. Think of it as breaking and entering, Nick, to reach his loved one.' He chuckled, and I felt myself smiling, though more at the strangeness of all this than at the joke. 'Now, let's consider the moment

173

when he's found her, and they've climbed for hours and hours, up through the darkness, with the ghosts of the dead people clutching at their heels. She's just behind him. The only thing is: he mustn't look back. That's the bargain. If he looks back, he'll lose her. And just as he gets to the daylight, he's suddenly seized by doubt—what if it's all been a trick and she hasn't been following—and he turns round . . . Now . . .'

He leaned back in his chair, and clapped his hands. 'Work! No script, no costumes. *Be* it. Show me what the two of you can do.' Somewhere in the side of my brain a warning bell was ringing. This is it, the warning said. Another test. What if we'd got this far and failed?

The thought was there, but a long way away. As he'd been talking, the story had been coming back, screening itself in my head like a film. Now I found myself up on my feet, and it made my head spin, so I slowed down. As I moved towards Swan, it felt like walking underwater, and I couldn't help smiling. I was moving smoothly, as slow as a lizard, and it was no effort. This was the kind of feeling all of us were working for.

'Forget your routines,' said Dom behind us. 'Improvise. You *are* Orpheus. You, Eurydice. This is the moment. Suddenly it strikes you: what if she's not there? And he turns—very slowly—and there she is, but too late—very, very slowly being snatched away . . .'

I don't know what we did. I don't remember even thinking, But how can this made-up ballerina in a tutu be Eurydice? I remember the way my eyes panned very gradually along the wall of books, and each glossy spine seemed to quiver as I passed it, full of colours like a stained-glass window. I was turning, slowly, and a motionless Swan was sliding, slow as the moon in the night sky, into view. Dom was there too, in the corner of my eye, peering in, but for me it was Swan, just Swan

174

who mattered. Her fingers reached for mine, and as our eyes met, we were all there was in the world or ever would be. We were floating in time, or *on* time, because time had ceased to be a narrow stream but had spread itself out into an ocean, lapping and dark and gentle, rippling out in all directions as far as I could see. And all I had to do was float on it, and feel the slow, slow current moving both of us together, Swan and me.

And then the light had changed: it was darker in the skylight window. My body was stiff and sore, with dull muscle fatigue all over, though I couldn't make out why. Swan's hand and mine were touching, still raised in that gesture that was half a greeting, half farewell, with the tips of our fingers entwined.

I moved first. She seemed to blink and see me for the first time, then she blushed and looked away. But she was smiling. I was smiling too.

'Good,' Dom said. 'Sit down.' I sank into the armchair with a grateful sigh. 'Extraordinary,' he said. 'You must have sensed it. I can see you did. Tell me, what *did* you feel?'

I looked at Swan. She was staring at me, with her mouth a little open, as if she didn't quite believe what she'd seen.

'Did it feel . . . good?' Dom prompted. We both nodded. 'Did it feel . . . closer to happiness than you have ever been?'

Swan spoke. 'Yes,' she said in a small voice.

'I could see it,' said Dom. 'And never, never have you statued better. But I have a small confession. Forgive me.' He paused, and leaned a little forward. 'The drink,' he said, 'contained a little, just a little, of a certain preparation. There is a lichen that grows in the tundra, sometimes alongside the cloudberries, that the shamans of the tribes there used to use.'

175

'You mean, a drug?' I said.

He tilted his head, not a yes or a no. 'A preparation. When you say *drug*, people imagine being drunk. That, or crazy visions. Didn't you see . . . exactly what was there? All that changed was the speed. Or the slowness. What does Antonin call it—Mind of Stone?'

Something brushed through my mind like a cold wind. I looked at Swan; she was nodding, hanging on his every word. My body was calm, and warm, and slightly floating. The cold wind was a memory of Maisie, whispering: *Once you've felt it, nothing else will do.* And that phrase again, that I kept hearing and I'd not quite understood: was this *going for stone* . . . ?

'It was a mild dose,' Dom said. 'But feeling it is the only way to understand.' Somewhere back in the building, there was knocking on a door, which became a banging, then abruptly stopped. 'Let me explain. For the standards my clients demand, mere practice is not good enough. Even the astonishing Antonin would hardly satisfy. They want something almost superhuman, so close to the borderline of flesh and stone that you can scarcely tell. With a careful use of this preparation—as the shamans did—almost superhuman feats of slowness and control are possible. And you must agree: it has its incidental pleasures, no?'

Swan was nodding. Dom looked at me. Back in the house there was the sound of voices, raised. Dom frowned. 'Excuse me,' he said. 'I'll leave you to discuss it for a moment.' Standing up, he pushed the table with the bottle and the glasses closer to us, and I noticed that he'd hardly sipped his, after all. He laid one hand on Swan's shoulder, one on mine. 'The special thing, the very special thing, is that it's both of you. Believe me: nothing less will do.'

20

It was coincidence, of course—the knocking on the door, and the raised voices in the corridor, and the way Dom happened to put down the bottle with the preparation just between us, in arm's reach. It might have been . . . but I'm not sure that anything happened just by chance in Dom's world. Whatever, he'd gone out into some anteroom, to help his two tough guys sort out the bother, and he'd left us in the study with the preparation on the table in between.

I looked at Swan, and saw her looking at it. And I realized that she couldn't take her eyes away. Now she was reaching out her hand . . .

'No!' I said. 'Don't touch it.'

She blinked and looked up as if I'd disturbed a good daydream. 'What?' she said, and for a moment she looked like a little girl caught in the act, all pout and defiance: *why shouldn't I if I want to?*

'God knows what that stuff is. It's powerful.'

'You bet . . . ' she said, and smiled. It was the smile that scared me—like a person with a special secret.

'Swan! You know about . . . drugs and stuff.' I remembered her arms, and shuddered. 'You know what they do to you.'

'So?' she said sharply. 'And what do *you* know?' We were whispering, but each whisper felt loud as a shout. Outside, somewhere down the corridor, there were two voices now: Dom's, quieter, and Antonin's, rising sharp and shrill.

177

'Not much . . . ' I faltered. 'But enough.' I had to keep a grip. It might have been the comedown from the dose we'd just had, but my mind seemed to be moving in judders, like a jerky film. 'I know that if anything feels that good, you'll want to do it again.'

'So you *do* want to . . . ' she said, suddenly bright-eyed. 'Look, he's left it out for us. Just a drop . . . ' She took my hand, maybe to guide it to the bottle. 'It gets better, second time.'

You can tell that my brain was still slow; it took a second or two to hit me, what she'd said.

This hadn't been her first time . . . When . . . ? Yes, she'd been up here yesterday. ' . . . with him. You did that with him, didn't you? The same routine? Gazing into his eyes too, like that?'

For a moment I thought she was going to hit me. Then she softened. 'No,' she said. 'Look, I did my act for him. That's all. Nick, try to understand. OK, I was into some bad scenes when I was younger. But this is . . . different.'

'Oh yeah? Isn't that what they always say? And . . . ' The thoughts were falling into place, one by one. 'You planned it, didn't you? With him.' She didn't answer. 'You did, didn't you? You had it all lined up for me, and I fell into it.'

'You forced your way in! Broke in, like a burglar.' She stopped, out of breath and trembling. I knew I was trembling too.

'I came for you,' I said.

The blaze had gone from her eyes. 'Nick, Nick . . . You might not like Dom . . . But surely you can see: this isn't just about some high? It's . . . '

'Business,' I said. 'His business.'

'*Ours*,' she said. 'Our business. Nick, this is our chance. We've got to work together, Nick. You've got to help. I can't carry you. Don't be . . . a passenger . . . Nick?'

I don't know what she'd seen on my face, but she was leaning forward. 'Nick, you look strange. Are you OK?'

I was OK. I'd just remembered something, that's all, and it was like a little earthquake in my head. It was those words: *a passenger*. What I saw was Mum and Dad together, rounding on each other at the dining table. Him, slumped there, his head in his hands. He'd had another job interview, or rather he should have, but he hadn't gone. He'd been out of work for a year, and he was finding it harder to get out of bed, let alone go out and face a bunch of jumped up prats, he said, to beg for half the salary he should be earning. That's when she lost her cool and said one of those things that once you've said them they can never be unsaid. 'I do all the work in this family,' she'd said. 'You're just a passenger.' His face went very pale and wooden, and he didn't speak. The next morning, he was gone.

'Nick?' Swan said. 'Sorry, sorry.' She had both hands on my shoulders now, and kept them there until I met her eyes. 'Listen to me,' she said. 'Two things . . . One: we've got to do this. Do you think I'm going back downstairs to be like all the others? This is the only chance there is.' She was speaking fast and softly. 'Two—and I'm not going to talk about this, there's no time . . . Two: back there, just now, was *wonderful*, the best thing ever . . . because it was *you*.'

That's when I knew that I would say yes in the end . . . to whatever it was. I'm not proud of it. Somehow all the fight had gone out of me, just like that. 'OK,' I said. 'So it doesn't matter that we don't know what his business is? That stuff out there in the attic, I bet that's not legal. Smuggling art treasures in from abroad—you hear about it on the news. It's not innocent art lovers who do it, it's gangs—a nice sideline from the drugs trade. What are we getting into?'

179

At the end of the corridor, Antonin's voice was suddenly shrill and angry. Then Dom's voice, quiet. Then Antonin's, rising again. And they were coming closer.

'If that was a mild dose,' I said, 'what's a *big* one like?' Then it hit me. 'Matty . . . Matty the Pan. Is *that* what did his head in?'

'He couldn't handle it. Had the wrong attitude. But we've got each other.' Swan reached out, picked up Dom's glass, and sniffed the un-drunk preparation. 'Come on,' she said. 'I'm not frightened. Are you?' Her eyes were bright now, though I think her hand was trembling slightly. 'And I know what I'm doing.' She took a sip, then put the glass down firmly. 'See? I know what I'm doing.' Then for an instant there was something younger, almost child-like in her eye. 'Oh, Nick, whatever happens . . . stick with me.'

The door banged open. Antonin strode in, like a man who's been out in a high wind. 'Enough!' he said. 'I am summoned. OK, OK! I come. Am I one of the servants?' Dom was just behind him. Antonin noticed us and swept us a low bow. I could see, though, he was quivering with emotion, and his eyes were blazing darker than I'd ever seen. 'I am not your servant. I am an artist. An *artiste*. I think you forget that. It is too long that I put up with this treatment. I demand respect!'

Dom glanced at Swan and me, with a look that said: *one of his tantrums* . . . I guessed it wasn't the first time, the way Dom sighed. 'Monsieur Asch,' he said. 'Everyone here respects you. You are the greatest artist of your kind.'

'Words. Hah!' Antonin snapped his fingers. 'So much for your words. You use my expertise. My discipline. My inspiration. Then you call for me, like a servant. Then you put me in the fault. Respect? Maybe you forget: I am the genius; you are just a tradesman. Yes, a tradesman, even if you do your trade with gangsters with their drugs and guns.'

There was a hush, and I think Dom glanced in our direction, just an instant, to see if we had registered what we'd heard. I didn't move or blink. In that moment, though, I saw what made him so successful in his world of shady dealings. He wasn't so much the doctor with a bedside manner; more the senior civil servant—cool, controlled, discreet. 'Monsieur Asch,' Dom said, 'you have made your point. You must be practical. Tell me what you are asking for.'

'Yes, I am practical. If this respect of yours is real, give me the proof.'

'What proof?'

'My own statue. For once . . . ' Antonin's voice dropped. Suddenly it had an unnerving sweetness in it. 'All these young things I prepare for you . . . For once, give me a statue I shall care for. One statue, is all, of my very own.' He smiled, a deliberate mime smile, too long and too wide. 'If not . . . ' The smile snapped off his face. 'I go. No more statues for you. End of the whole charade.'

There was a stillness, as the two men faced each other.

'I know this is nothing to you but a calculation,' said Antonin. 'Numbers on a balance sheet. What do they cost, these children? Nothing. Whose work is it that makes them worth money for you? Mine. So it costs nothing to spare one for me.'

Dom looked at him coldly. Maybe inside his head there was a calculation, because then he gave a weary sigh. 'Very well,' he said. 'I'll find you one.'

'Hah! As my benevolent employer chooses! No, just this once . . . it happens *as it pleases me*.'

'All right, all right.' Dom was losing his cool now,

though only the slightest quiver passed across his face. Antonin would have seen it. 'Go downstairs right now,' said Dom. 'Choose one.'

'Hah!' said Antonin slowly. 'You think second best will do. If you thought any of them *downstairs* was the best, you would have them for yourself. Like these . . . ' He panned that stare over Swan and me. 'Like *her*.'

'Sorry . . . ' Dom said. 'Not her.' That's when Antonin exploded. With a leap I could scarcely believe for his age, he was beside us. He had Swan by the arm.

'So . . . ' he crowed, watching Dom's face intently. 'You want her, do you? She is your perfect work of art? You reject so many others that I send you, and you choose her. Well . . . ' And he started to laugh. He laughed slowly, deliberately, in Dominic's face. 'And what if she is not so perfect?' He reached into his pocket and for a second I had a vision of him pulling out something terrible, a knife or worse, but no: what he held was a lace-bordered hanky. He held it up, like the conductor of an orchestra. 'What,' said Antonin, 'if you are the short-sighted one?' He yanked Swan's arm up, spat a great gob on it and scrubbed with the hanky at the paint inside the elbow and the wrist. He jerked her round and held it out for Dom to see— exposed, where the stage paint had hidden it, the needle marks, the scar. Dom flinched, and Antonin saw it. 'Not so perfect, no? See, she is damaged goods!'

And that was it, that phrase, the bottom line. All the kids downstairs, doing their aerobics, working out, checking their faces for the slightest spot. Swan, in a panic when she heard Dom, slapping the make-up on her arms. And Maisie . . . It wasn't because Antonin had *hurt* her Dom got angry, it was *leaving marks* he couldn't stand. I thought of what they say about secret police, how the art is not to leave traces that show.

Dom was looking at Swan—a slow look, up and down,

and very cold. Disappointment? It wasn't that personal. She was damaged goods, and that was all.

'Please . . . ' Swan started.

'Stop her mouth,' Dom said. Antonin's hand clapped tight over her mouth. I was halfway to my feet, but one of Dom's men, the one he'd called Jarvis, appeared beside me like a shadow and his hand fell on my shoulder. Dom had taken a step forward, stooping slightly to look at Swan. 'Take her away,' he said, quietly.

'No!' I lunged forward but the man's hands clamped round both my arms. As I struggled, Antonin bowed, theatrically, jerking Swan down with him. She didn't resist, and when he snapped upright she straightened up slower, rather awkwardly. What was the matter with her? Of course: the extra sip from Dom's glass that she'd taken for bravado. How much had there been in it? *It's better second time*, she'd said. How much effect would it have?

'Thank you,' said Antonin. 'I shall look after her. I shall reward your faith . . . and show you something *perfect*, after all!' As they moved towards the door she wrenched her head free and strained back towards me, then with a tug he hauled her out into the corridor. The man eased me down in the chair.

'Stop him!' I said. 'He's a psycho.' I looked at Dom but he had no expression. 'Don't you care?'

'I'm sorry about that,' said Dom, as if I hadn't spoken. For the first time, I thought, he was rattled, though hardly a quiver of it showed on his face. 'An unnecessary scene. I can't abide it when things have to get . . . physical.'

'It's not her fault,' I said.

'No, no, indeed. It's myself I blame. A lapse of judgement.' He turned to me. 'Your friend deceived me, but she was only doing what comes naturally—to her kind, I mean. Did you know about her?'

What would Swan's advice be? I could almost hear

183

her whisper in my ear: *No choice. Go along with it. Don't rile him*. So I shook my head. Still, I hated myself for it.

'Most of them are damaged,' he said, half to himself. 'And desperate, too. Disposable people. Though you . . . I can't be sure. You seem different.'

'*You* gave her the drug,' I said. 'Like Matty. Is that what happened to him?' I'd started, and I couldn't stop. I knew they weren't sensible questions to be asking. The hand was still heavy on my shoulder but, to my surprise, Dom nodded towards the door. The hand released its grip.

'Matty . . . Was he your friend too?' Dom sat down beside me. 'No, I thought not. He lacked the mental strength, did Matty. And if you don't have the discipline, the kind Antonin's training provides, the effects of the preparation can as easily be Hell as Heaven. The Pan simply panicked. There was nothing I could do with him then.'

'But he still wanted more,' I said. The thought was horrible. Matty had been craving, twitching, for the drug that might send him back to Hell. 'Is that what it does? It's that addictive?'

'People do get a taste for it,' said Dom blandly, and behind his casual gesture I saw just how the life of a Gloria would be. You could leave when you liked, Dom had said. Except that your new employer—no, he'd let the real word slip out earlier: *owner*—would have the drug, which imprisoned you, surer than locks and chains. 'Weak people, that is,' he said. 'The stronger-minded can simply enjoy it. I take a drop myself for recreation now and then.' As he spoke, he measured a little of the liquid into a new glass. 'It is a unique experience, don't you agree? There . . . ' He laid the glass down on the table next to me. 'You are angry now. It does you credit. But what I am offering you is the best life you could hope to have.'

So this was the choice. What were the options? I could

184

take the stuff and dash it in his face. Or . . . There was Swan's voice again in my mind saying: *Go along with it. You've got no choice.*

And yet I mustn't seem desperate—one of his disposable people. I frowned, as if I was really thinking. 'Two things . . . ' I said. 'One . . . '

'Well, well . . . ' Dom had a half-amused look on his face now. People didn't make conditions with him very often. I couldn't guess what happened if they tried.

'Swan . . . ' I said. 'Tell Antonin not to hurt her.'

For a moment I thought I'd blown it. Dom gazed at the ceiling, then sighed. 'I don't think Antonin will hurt the Swan. I hurt his pride a little, that was all. But if it will set your mind at rest . . . ' He glanced to the doorway, where the man who'd been holding me was waiting. 'Jarvis, keep an eye on Monsieur Asch, will you?' he said. 'Just make sure he doesn't get carried away. Thank you. Now . . . ' Dom turned back to me. 'Rest assured that when Jarvis has an order, then the thing gets done. But what about you? What was your second thing?'

I took a breath. *You'll understand, Swan, won't you?* I was thinking in my head. 'I don't want this to be the end of our deal, just because Swan's dropped out. Can you find another girl for me?'

'Well, well . . . ' said Dom, with an arch of his eyebrows. 'A man after my own heart. I've been under-estimating you. I think we have a deal.'

'Cheers,' I said, and raised the glass to my lips.

185

21

When I was small, there was one particular medicine I couldn't stand: Doctor Gulliver's Herbal Linctus. It was something herbal and organic, that Mum thought was a good idea. It tasted like a cross between a bonfire and a compost heap. It was on those nights when I had a slight cough and Mum leaned over the bed with the Dr Gulliver's that I perfected my one and only conjuring trick. I just hoped my old instinct wouldn't desert me, because I hadn't done it for years.

What you do is this. When I was ill in bed, I'd always have a wad of tissues handy. You bunch them up in one hand, then reach up with the other, coughing a bit to create a diversion. You take the glass in both hands, cradling it, so the tissues get between the glass and your chin. Now with the rim of the glass just on your lip—you might need to cough a bit more here—you tilt it just enough, so that it looks as if you're drinking, and the liquid dribbles down into the tissue, and if you pour it at the right speed and the tissue's big enough . . . it doesn't drip. But you need a diversion.

'Isn't that Antonin there?' I said, looking at the CCTV screen that showed the garden. Dom only glanced a moment, just long enough to say no, but by that time I was setting the glass down, empty. 'Yeuch.' I made a face, like I'd done with the first taste. Just the memory of it was enough.

Clunk: I dropped the glass, and as it teetered, Dom

couldn't help looking. At the same time my other hand had slipped down behind my chair, dropping the wad of sodden tissue.

'Hey . . . ' I said. 'This stuff's strong.' I got to my feet. 'Do you want me to do the act? It felt brilliant last time.'

'Oh, enjoy yourself.' Dom looked pleased now. 'This one's on the house—just so you know you've made the right decision.'

I was walking now, not quite naturally—the way you do in a shoe shop when you're trying on a new pair. And I was thinking. How long had it been last time, before it started working? Almost straight away, I thought. I had to get it right: Dom was watching me closely. 'Hey . . . ' I said again, and let the word slur slightly. 'I can feel it. Hey, that's weird . . . ' I looked down at my hand. Last time there'd been a moment when I noticed this hand moving, in the corner of my eye, making its gesture really slowly, and it was only when I traced it up the arm that I realized it was mine. And I had to be slowing, slowing it, now . . .

It was the hardest statue act I'd ever done . . . and with no practice. Antonin once said *You have it*. I prayed he was right.

Why hadn't I looked around more carefully—spied out all the exits—when I had the chance? But it was too late now. I knew there was a corridor; that's where the knocking had been, and it must be the main door down into the house. No use thinking of that: Dom's second man was waiting out there. At the other end of the room was the door I'd come through, back into the warehouse-attic. If I could get there . . . But how far away was it? Going into a slow, slow gesture now—I was Orpheus again, reaching out to an invisible Eurydice—I let my eyes track past it, and my heart sank. It was too far. Another time, I could have walked there in a few strides, but not at

187

this speed. Why hadn't I thought, and made sure I was closer before starting to slow down?

As my slow gesture panned me round, I felt Dom just beside me, watching every move. Every step, every blink had to be right now, with just the right sort of slowness. After all, he was the expert, wasn't he—the connoisseur? Now we were next to the packing case on the pallet, and for a moment I was eye to eye with the Buddha. He had flaking gold all over him, and such a sad knowing smile on his face. I know, it's tough, he seemed to say. And behind him were the doors—more like a cupboard than a doorway—which must be where they'd winched the pallet up from the courtyard outside.

Of course. How else had they got the statues up here? Some of them were too big to carry upstairs. There must be a hoist or a lift or something out there. And the doors were only fastened with a single bolt. I let the sweep of my hand take me round further—just half a turn, so slowly that the muscles of my legs cried out—and as I went I felt Dom circling with me, so close I could feel his breath. And as I turned I let my weight sink into my knees. Now to tremble a little; now for a shudder, as if I might fall. Dom took a step towards me, with his arms out, and I let myself drop to a crouch, my balance to the back leg, ready for the moment.

Now.

I lunged. I went into him hard, my shoulder aimed straight at his solar plexus. It winded him, so though his mouth was open no sound came. I straightened and pulled him up with me, forcing his head back with a crack against the wall. That ought to have knocked him out cold, but he was tough, for all he looked the smoothie. Any second, he'd scream. I yanked him around and got an arm around his throat, and pulled until he gagged. He struggled, but I held on.

If this had been an action movie, I guess I'd have strangled him, as cool as that. Do you have any idea how hard that really is? I let him fall towards me, then rammed him backwards, and the flimsy doors fell open with hardly a thud. There we were, all at once, with damp air on our faces, in the open air. I held my breath, waiting for the heavy to come bursting into the room behind us, raising the alarm. He didn't. We'd been that quick, and that quiet, and that lucky. Lucky? When I looked down at my feet, I wasn't sure.

I'd expected a lift-shaft, at least. What I got was a scaffolding platform, just wide enough to swing a pallet onto. Over our heads was the hook of the pulley, but no lift, no way down except to fall. One slip, we'd both be over. I strained his head forward to make sure he could see. There was the courtyard, two storeys down—a square U-shape, with the lower stable block on one side and the workshops on the other. Just behind the workshop roof, a cloud of dust and smoke rose up, and the sneering sound of the stone saw.

Dom wasn't struggling now. He'd gone rigid. 'Pl . . . please . . . ' he whimpered with the little bit of breath I left him. 'Inside . . . Please . . . A-afraid of heights.' And for a crazy moment I could have burst out laughing: this was the man who talked about his *disposable people* . . . Out here, without his bodyguards, without his money, Dom was a quivering heap. No wonder he didn't like things *getting physical*.

All that, and it was coming on to rain.

'What do you want?' he whispered. 'Money? I'll do anything.'

'Dead right,' I said, 'you will.' The only trouble was . . . What did I want to do? I hadn't planned this. I had no idea. Whatever happened now, it had to happen fast. Should I steer him back in through the window, back into

189

the corridor, where the bodyguard was waiting? Or should I leave him to it, and find my own way down somehow? No, if he managed to raise the alarm, how many people would be waiting by the time I reached the ground? Like it or not, I needed Dom with me. He was the only bargaining card I'd got. For a moment I was almost sorry for him . . . then I got the flashback. *Trash!* he'd said. *Damaged goods* and given Swan away. At that moment I could have said *Good riddance* as I pushed him off the edge.

But I didn't. 'For a start,' I said, 'I want Swan. And . . .' The breath stopped in my throat. The courtyard was empty, or that's what I'd thought, but just outside the workshop door was a shape, something moving, that I couldn't quite make out looking down from this angle. It moved in jerks, and it gave me a bad feeling. I needed to see what it was.

'Move!' I whispered in Dom's ear. There was a narrow ledge, a knee-high parapet. Somewhere there must be a fire escape or something—maybe just out of sight round the corner of the roof. On my own I could have walked it, but the two of us . . . 'One foot at a time,' I said. Dom was still stiff but he didn't resist, and like two puppets in a dance we shuffled sideways. On one side, the slates of the roof rose steeply, glinting with rain. On the other side, the small lip, and the drop. What if he panicked? I took a breath and edged us on.

A few metres to the corner now . . . and a gust of wind hit us. We staggered, stumbling sideways against the roof. Dom would have stayed there, flattened against the wet slates, but I pulled him upright. I was rattled now, but we had to keep moving, or we'd both freeze up with fear. I made myself look down, into the courtyard.

I saw Jarvis. That was what the shape in the workshop doorway was—not one figure but two, and they were struggling with each other. Then one fell away, and it was

Jarvis stretched out on the cobbles, limp. The other figure straightened up and it didn't take a second look to tell me it was Antonin.

'Stop him,' I said to Dom. 'You're meant to be the boss round here.' He stiffened. Bracing myself, I leaned him forward. I had one of his arms crooked up behind his back now. My other hand was on his collar, forcing him forwards. 'Shout,' I said.

'A-Antonin,' said Dom, faintly. No way would they hear above the noise of the stone saw.

'Antonin!' I yelled, as loud as I could. It worked. The figure below looked round, looked up.

'Now!' I said.

'St . . . stop,' called Dom feebly. 'That . . . that's an order.'

For a moment Antonin's face looked up towards us, very still. Then he laughed.

'I am not your servant,' he shouted, when the laughter waned. 'I am an artist. Wait and see.' Next moment he was dragging the limp weight of Jarvis with him; the workshop door slammed, and Antonin was gone.

Dom was breathing in little gasps now, like a kid who's just stopped crying. He'd got past the struggling stage and felt as feeble as a person in a fever: that's what panic does for you. 'We're going down,' I said and peered round the corner. There wasn't a fire escape, just a sheer drop to the glass roof of the conservatory, and not even a ledge. Then I spotted the answer, down by our feet. It wasn't the answer I'd been hoping for. There was just an iron ladder that came straight up the wall and ended in a couple of iron loops for handholds at the top. Below—not far below, maybe only three metres—was the steep roof of the stables. I had to work this out. 'OK,' I said. 'You first.'

That was a mistake. I had to turn him round so he'd face inwards, and the moment I released his arm he

191

grabbed at me like a drowning man. For a second I thought he was going to wrestle me down, then make a break for it, but no . . . His arms clamped round me, and we staggered, coming to our knees. I grabbed at the ladder. 'Help me, damn you,' I said, but he was past it, sobbing like a frightened child. I was going to have to do this by myself. As I swung myself out on the ladder, feeling for the rungs, his dead weight came with me, and cold iron bit into my fingers as I held, and held . . . I didn't let go. No, the ladder gave way, rusted bolts wrenching out of their fixtures, and the whole thing peeled off slowly, twisting as it came.

It was the slowness that saved us, though all I felt was the thump that struck me almost sideways as we hit the stable roof. Then we were slithering, together, with part of the ladder underneath us, grating down the mossy slates. Then we'd thudded into something at another angle and, amazingly, were still. We should have been sprawled on the cobbles of the courtyard, dead. We weren't. As I opened my eyes the crazy angles sorted into some sense of up and down. The ladder had wedged in a gully where the main roof met the small roof of a dormer window, just enough to hold our weight. Dom groaned. His eyelids flickered. How badly he was hurt, I couldn't tell. He'd been underneath when we struck, and cushioned me. If there'd been time, I might even have said: thanks, mate. Dom had helped me after all.

I left him in the cradle of the buckled ladder. Somewhere beneath me, Swan must be. With Antonin. Don't think of that. Just get there. I got my hands on the edge of the dormer and eased myself down. There was a ledge, a foothold, and—luck, luck was with me—the little window was open a crack. One kick, it came wide open. I swung my legs in and slithered over the window ledge, knocking over a shelf-full of bottles, not caring, and

192

grating my arm on the catch as I crumpled panting on to a cold tiled floor.

There was a scream, and several things happened together. I grabbed the nearest thing—a wash-basin—and pulled myself up to my knees. As I did, I saw an apparition in the mirror. It was a wild-haired man, with wild eyes, wet, his clothes all torn and smeared like camouflage colours with mud and moss, and a bloodstain trickling from somewhere. That was me.

At the same time, a door had banged open, and someone screamed. Somewhere behind her, there was a sound of a toilet still flushing. Laura-Lee stood there, with her mouth wide open, and the scream died away as she saw, I guess, that it was me. At least she must have seen that it wasn't a rapist or murderer, but someone battered, dazed, and aching, on his knees. I opened my arms, palms up, and waited for everyone to come running. It could have been a gesture of defeat.

But no one came. She stared at me, dumbstruck, and she didn't scream again.

'You've got to help,' I gasped. 'It's Antonin. He's got Swan.' Laura-Lee swayed in the doorway, caught between the urge to listen or to run. 'He attacked Jarvis,' I said. 'Yes, really! I think he's got her in the workshop.'

'In the workshop?' That was when I saw the shadow of alarm behind her eyes.

'What's he doing?' I said. 'He was shouting something about *a perfect work of art* . . . What is it?' I said. Laura-Lee was shaking her head, and there was a wild look in her eyes. She knew something. She'd been here longest. Better than anyone here except Dom, she knew his history.

His history. I had an icy feeling.

'1968,' I said. 'When he was locked away . . . What had he done? What was the *shocking incident*?'

She was shaking her head. *No,* it was saying, *no, no, no!*

193

'Tell me! What did he do?' I was on my feet now, with my hands on her arms. There was Antonin's voice in my head: *the perfect work of art,* he was saying. There he was with a statue, planting a real kiss on its cold stone lips. 'Tell me! It's the Venus de Milo, isn't it?' Inside my grip, I felt her stiffen. 'That's it, isn't it?'

I must have been shaking her, but she didn't resist. 'OK . . . Steps of the Louvre . . . May '68, you know . . . It was a kind of protest . . . against Art . . . '

'What did he do?'

She looked up, and her eyes met mine. 'He made one,' she whispered. 'A Venus de Milo.'

'Go on.' I knew. In my mind I saw Swan's arms. The flaw. The one thing about her that stopped her from being perfect. I knew, but Laura-Lee had to say it. She wasn't a monster. If she said it out loud, she'd be bound to help me. 'Say it, Laura-Lee, please. Out loud.'

'He used . . . he used a real girl.' And in that moment I saw the workshop—just the glimpse I'd had when I peered in. I saw the workbench and the tools, and everything that had seemed like a sick dream was suddenly very cool and clear and true.

'Dom tried to stop him,' I said. 'He gave him an order, straight out. Antonin just laughed.' I could see she was wavering. 'You've got to choose,' I said. 'Dom or Antonin. Which will it be?'

'Where's Dom?' said Laura-Lee.

'Upstairs. There's no time.' On the roof above our head there was a little scratching sound, like mice or birds. She noticed it, and looked up, but before she could ask there was another, harsher sound.

In the depths of the building was a whine, a sneering sound that started, faltered, then rose to a *wheee!* like a child on a ride at a theme park. It was the stone saw.

'Quick!' I said.

She closed her eyes and took a breath. Then she nodded. 'OK.'

22

I would never have known there was a back way
without Laura-Lee. I'd have headed for the courtyard,
and . . . sometimes I wake up in the night and
think about it. What if I'd got there too late? As she led
me down the back stairs, the whine of the stone saw in
the yard had dropped, but as we came to the workshop
door it was louder. Laura-Lee rattled the handle, then
hammered—once, twice—though there wasn't much
point, with that noise. I took a step back and barged. The
hinges gave way with a rip. As the door fell inwards, I
stared round, trying not to think what I might see.

In the long room the light from the windows was
dimmed by dust and cobwebs. Framed in one, there was
the stonemason, deaf and unspeaking, Antonin's old
friend, working in a cloud of stone dust in the yard. With
the faded dusty look on everything, it could have been a
postcard of some rural craft in times gone by. He was
alone, head down in his goggles, with his back to us, as
unperturbed as ever, while the saw bit and relaxed and bit
again with a rising and falling screech. It was his
calmness that was eerie—just like any working day. The
Place was exploding in violence around him, but he was
as far away as a diver working on the ocean bed.

Swan wasn't out there—that was something. When
I'd heard the saw, I'd thought . . . No, I didn't even want
to think what I'd thought. But where was she? I looked
round in the gloom. No sign of her, or Jarvis, or . . .

'No!' It was Laura-Lee, just behind me, and I turned to

196

see Antonin, just in time, as he came at me. In the same flash I saw Swan, in the corner behind him, slumped on a hard chair, but even that glimpse nearly cost us the game, because I missed the flash of the chisel in Antonin's grip. Laura-Lee saw it, though, and she put out a hand. There was a little spray of blood and she staggered back, mouth wide open. Any sound she was making was drowned by the noise of the saw. I jumped aside as Antonin slashed again; there was the flash of the chisel tip, just a hand's breadth from my face, then I crashed into the shelves, which shuddered. Jars of nails, paint cans, and nameless tool shed things were raining down around me, and that might have been what slowed him for a second, just enough. All I know is that I grabbed the first thing like a weapon—something large to fend off blows—something made of wood and wire and metal—and I swung it at him as he lunged and crunch, it caught him, and he staggered. Only as I swung it again, hardly pausing in the movement, did I realize what it was: Albie's child-automaton, the one Antonin had broken in the courtyard. He was off balance, and it caught him in the face. As he fell, the chisel slipped from his grip, and I kicked it away. Then I slammed with the manikin, down, and again and again, until his arm wasn't coming up to shield his head any more, and I hit him, until he wasn't moving, and just to make sure I hit him again.

Laura-Lee was crouched, cradling one arm with the other, staring at the blood that spilled between her fingers. But I couldn't think of her, just now. I ran to Swan.

She was limp in her chair, tied upright while her arms hung at her sides. They were bare, and with a shudder I saw a thin red line round each, like the mark left by a child's sundress with elasticated sleeves. Antonin had felt-penned it in, like surgeons do before the cut.

I forced myself to look up. On the bench, beneath a

197

cobwebbed window, spread on what might have been a tablecloth or dustsheet, were . . . I couldn't look. There were implements, I know, and he must have been sharpening them with a grindstone, because there was a glint of wicked edges, and there was an old enamel bowl of water and . . . I looked away. I've read about what doctors used to do on board ship in the olden days. I threw my arms round Swan and held her tight, tight, tight.

'Are you OK?' I said. 'Say something.' There was no reply. Her mouth hung open slightly, as if she'd been screaming till she was exhausted. Antonin hadn't even bothered to gag her, with the noise of the saw to do the job.

I was down on my knees now, arms around her, and her eyelids flickered open. Then she seemed to gulp and try to speak, but if any sound came it was too faint to hear. Just behind her, a black extension cable ran from a power point on the wall. I grabbed it with both hands and tugged, and the saw cut out, its high screech falling to a fading whine. As it did, I smoothed my hand down the side of her face, and something—the state of shock, or the drug, or both—seemed to let go its hold on her. She looked up and as if she'd seen me for the first time, she began to weep.

The door from the courtyard came open, and there was the stonemason, pushing up his goggles, squinting in the half-light. After a moment he seemed to make out me and Swan, then Laura-Lee, and a slight frown of puzzlement, maybe, crossed his face. Then he caught sight of Antonin, crumpled, and his mouth came open in a silent wail. Next moment he was kneeling beside him, lifting his head gently, mopping his forehead, smoothing down his thin grey hair.

Swan was struggling up now, looking pale and faint with shock. Her legs buckled, and I caught her. Then I saw the wheelbarrow—the one they'd loaded Matty into—and I backed her round and eased her down. It was as deep as a small bathtub. 'It's all right,' I breathed in her ear, 'it's all right. I'll get you out of here.' It was more for my own sake than hers. For a moment she tried to sit up, but she was weak and shivering. She let me fold her arms and legs in, till she was curled up like a sleeping child. She trusted me.

As we got to the open door a gust of wet wind hit me. I looked round for something to cover her up; there was a pile of old torn plastic sheeting on the workshop floor. As I tugged at the top piece it came away easily and I saw what was beneath it: Jarvis, with a pool of dark blood by his head.

There are times when you don't stop and look, just move. Any moment Laura-Lee would shout, or the stonemason raise the alarm, or the other bodyguard would go into the attic and find us gone, or someone would notice Dom up on the roof. Whatever happened, I wanted us out of it. I wished Hob was there, to give us tips on disappearing now. I tucked the plastic round Swan. Then we were out in the courtyard, cursing the rain but grateful, too: at least there'd be no one out strolling. As I made for the gate I was thinking: how was I going to blag it? Couldn't I just say that I was a gardener, with a load of stuff for . . . ? No, I didn't have a story, but my feet kept walking. Then I came round the corner of the building, and I saw it was too late for stories anyway.

All the floodlights whacked on, and the drive and gate were washed with cold white light. Back in the house an alarm bell started shrilling. All we could do was make for cover . . . but not fast. Run, and we'd be spotted. Walk like a gardener, I thought. In my mind I saw the stonemason's slow plod, and I plodded like him, slow, unruffled, round the corner of the building, out on to the terrace. In the shadows there, I rammed the barrow on to the grass where the lawn sloped downhill, and began to run.

Then it was farce, as well as panic. The barrow bucked and skidded, slewing sideways. My feet slipped on the mud. I sprawled; Swan slithered out. She was on her feet now, and we leaned against each other. I looked up the hillside and for the second time was thankful for the rain. A fine veil of drizzle was drifting off the lake. The houselights were a bright blur in the mist.

We were almost at the ha-ha. I kicked the barrow into the brambly ditch. The skidmarks would give us away if anybody thought to look, but I couldn't help that. The drop wasn't much, a metre or so, and we eased each other down, holding the brambles back where we could. I was scratched and bruised all over, but hardly felt it. I slithered down fast; she slumped against me, but she didn't lose her feet. I locked an arm around her and we stumbled, sometimes in sync, sometimes out, like an awful three-legged race.

She was shivering again. We needed shelter. Then I saw the boathouse. I didn't have a plan, except to get out of the rain. 'Don't stop,' I said. She shook her head. I caught her as her legs gave way. Inside, I bolted the door. Then I found a heavy box, a plank, and an oil drum and piled them against it, just in case. Only then did we let ourselves sink to the floor, our arms around each other. Both of us were shuddering.

Inside the boathouse it was dark at first. The only light came from the door-shaped opening at the lakeward end—just enough to make out each other's faces as our eyes got used to it. Then the world was still, with just the lap of water, and every now and then a hollow clunk. There was a boat in there, flat and square-ended: a punt. I didn't know much about punting, but the thing looked badly low in the water. The light was soft, reflected upwards from the water, filtered by the mist outside. I lay there, too tired to think.

'Nick?' Swan's voice was stronger now. 'Thanks.'

'Are you OK? You were . . . kind of *gone*. Out of it. Like that stuff hit you really strongly the second time round.'

'*Out of it* . . . Is that how it looks?' She paused. 'Nick, I wasn't. I couldn't move much but I could see—you remember how it was, when we both took it. And I could hear.' She shuddered. 'He kept talking, talking. I wanted to turn away or block my ears but . . . He was telling me what he was going to . . . Oh my God . . . ' Her voice faded. You get stories about life-support patients—how they've heard the doctors and their family discussing whether to switch them off. I imagine they come round with the same look in their eyes as Swan had now.

'Was he really . . . ' I said. 'Was he really going to . . . ?' The words wouldn't come out. 'He couldn't.'

She stared blankly for a moment. 'I don't know,' she said. 'He kept showing me the things, then he'd lean really close and whisper in my ear, then he'd step back and look at me, just . . . *look*. Nick, he could have done *anything*.' She shook her head as if to get rid of the thoughts. 'I tried to scream, but you can't. Remember how it felt when we did it together. How it felt like . . . *forever*?' I shut my eyes. Yes, time had stopped then; I could see how you'd yearn for it, that feeling. But to be like that in fear, in terror . . . ? 'That's what *stone* means, isn't it?' she said. 'Think of it . . . *forever*.' Then she sat upright, like the Swan I'd met first in the city, feisty and up for it.

'Well, what do we do now?' she said.

'Wait, I suppose. They've got their hands full up there. They won't be thinking about us.'

'Then?'

'Then when the fuss dies down . . . ' I trailed off. 'I

don't know.' She leaned against me and for a while we were still, with just the slap of water.

'Nick,' she said. 'I'm sorry.'

'What for?'

'I got you into this.'

'No, you didn't. You kept telling me to go home. You thought I was a spoiled kid.'

'Did I? I'm sorry, really sorry.'

'Look, stop saying that, OK?' There must have been an edge in my voice, because she looked up, puzzled.

'OK, OK,' she said. 'What's wrong with saying sorry? I *am* sorry.'

It must have been the tiredness, or the adrenalin still buzzing in my brain. 'It's a waste of time, that's why. People don't mean it. They just want to stop you minding. *Sorry*, they say. *Poor me, not my fault, look, can't you see I'm sorry . . .*'

'Nick,' said Swan. 'Who's saying this? It doesn't sound like you.'

That stopped me. What a cheek. But my voice had been rising; I could hear it hanging in the air. And she was right: it didn't sound like mine.

'Nick?' Swan said, and stopped in mid breath. She'd been going to say sorry again, and caught herself in time.

But it was all right. I knew whose the voice was. It was from years back. It had come from the telephone, out of those tiny earpiece holes. In the months after Dad left, I'd kept asking Mum about him. Where was he? When was he coming back? 'He's ill,' she'd said. 'He'll come back when he's better.' Once, I'd overheard her with a friend; the friend was asking, 'Is he getting help?' and Mum had got angry. 'He needs to stop feeling sorry for himself,' she'd said. 'I mean, Nick's more grown-up than that, and he's only a child.'

Then there'd been a day when Mum was out. The

202

phone went. At first I didn't recognize what I was hearing. I'd never heard a man's voice crying. *Sorry, sorry*, it was saying. How he hated himself for screwing all our lives up. How I must hate him; it was all his fault.

Then the money ran out. He'd been on a payphone. Maybe he tried to ring back, but he wouldn't have got through. I was still standing there, in the hallway, feeling sort of wooden, with the receiver in my hand, when Mum got home. She gave me an odd look, but I said I was dialling a friend; I'd forgotten the number. I thought I'd tell her later. Thinking back, I realized that I never did. She'd only have got angry or upset. And I was very grown-up, everybody said so, after all. But for years after that, whenever the phone went I'd make sure it wasn't me who answered it. I didn't want to hear that sound again.

Swan was looking at me, curiously, in the half light. 'Nick?' she said again.

'Nothing,' I said. I touched her face. 'I'm sorry too.'

The punt creaked and bumped at its mooring. I could hear her breathing, very close. That might be why I missed the sounds outside the boathouse. The first I knew, there was a rattling at the door.

23

We didn't breathe. There was silence, then the slow creak of a laugh I knew too well.

'I know you are there,' said Antonin, quite softly. 'I hear you talking. Maybe you intend to *do the decent thing* . . . ' It was a mockery of an English accent, and he laughed a little at his own joke. ' . . . like your friend Matty the Pan.'

It couldn't be him, surely? The way I'd hit him, he should be in hospital at least. Any normal man would . . . but this was Antonin. I thought of his face, so little flesh . . . those hollow eyes. With all these years of practice, maybe he was partly stone.

'You might as well do it,' said Antonin gently, through the crack in the door. 'Mister Dominic is very shaken up. If he catches you, do you think he will let either of you go? And my good friend the stonemason, he is most annoyed with you, young Amadeus. He has lent me his hammer. He desires me to crush you. First your fingers, then your hands, then . . . ' Antonin chuckled to himself a little. 'Or you might give me back the Swan. Then maybe I let you go.'

Swan tugged at my sleeve. I was frozen, my eyes on the door, but she tugged, and I looked where she was pointing. Could he get in, through the water door? Maybe not; it would be slippery and muddy, and I couldn't tell how deep. But he had a hammer. I stared at the crack of light in the door—he could smash his way through it, easily—and all the fight-and-flight in me went whoosh,

204

but I couldn't move a muscle. I just stared at that door. After all, where was there left to go?

'Come on!' Swan was shaking me, pulling me upright. She was pointing to the punt. It wobbled badly as I helped her in, then steadied, rocking gently, on slow waves that came in through the low arch from the lake. I just had time to fumble with the mooring. As the knot came free there was a crack behind us. I turned to see the wood around the door bolt splinter. For a moment the door jammed, then the oil drum clattered over and there was Antonin. Swan had the punt pole now; she braced it against the side and pushed. For a terrible moment the punt didn't move, then very gently it slid out, slowly at first then faster, as we ducked and we slid through the archway, out into the grey of the lake.

'Can you do this?' Swan grappled with the dripping pole.

I'd seen pictures but I'd never done it. Mostly I thought of cartoons, where the bloke gets the pole stuck and clings to it, like a monkey in a tree, while the punt drifts away. Still, I guessed I knew a little more than she did, so I balanced upright awkwardly. She sank to her knees and gazed back through the mist. I couldn't see Antonin. 'Push,' she said. 'What if he just wades?'

She was right. It wasn't very deep. I stayed low, with my feet wide, and I dug the pole in. It was heavy and dripping; as I tugged it back I nearly lost it, then I was digging it in, a little deeper, and I braced myself against it. We wobbled, side to side, but we were gathering speed.

The boathouse blurred and when I looked again the shore was gone. The mist was thicker out here on the lake. I'd had a thought in my mind that we could reach the other side, a place I'd never been, but the woods looked wilder. Maybe we could reach the outer wall that way.

Maybe. But which way was it? The last push with the

205

pole had slipped—we were in deeper water—and I felt us veering round, but how fast I couldn't tell. Before I could wrestle the pole out to push on the other side, we could have gone a hundred and eighty degrees.

Then there was Antonin, taunting. I couldn't make out words, but in the mist it was everywhere, somehow near yet far away. From somewhere else, too, equally far and nowhere, there were other voices calling. Were they looking for us, or for Antonin? Were they Dominic's henchmen, or the kids from the commune? And did it make any difference? With a sick feeling it hit me: yes, the others would be helping. I'd seen them in crit sessions, how they would savage each other, to please Antonin or Dom. I'd heard the gossip at mealtimes. I knew what they thought of Swan. Hob might be different, but where was he now? We'd better just accept that we were on our own.

If we could just get to the other side of the lake . . . I dug the pole in. It went down, down, and I staggered. Suddenly the bottom wasn't there. 'What's the matter?' Swan whispered, as I hauled the pole back in and shipped it.

'Can you swim?' I said.

'No.' We stared at each other. 'Can you?'

I nodded. 'Swim, then! Look, if Antonin gets to us . . . Or if Dom does, or . . . '

We drifted, silently. Were we moving at all? I had a feeling we were, slightly, but how could I tell? The water was flat, an even grey, without a ripple, and where it joined the flat grey mist I couldn't see. This was limbo, no place, no time—the kind of *forever* Swan had meant: the stone state, the kind of forever that had broken Matty's mind.

'Nick,' she said. 'I'm a mess. You know that. You'd have been better off not getting mixed up with me.' She held up her arms, with white paint dribbling off them, baring more of the evidence. Nervously, I reached out a finger, and touched. I didn't flinch. I looked her in the eye. 'Oh, Nick,' she said. 'Don't. Dom was right. This was the one chance, and I blew it. Just look after yourself, for Christ's sake. Go on, swim!'

We were eye to eye. I shook my head, quite slowly. Then she was staring up over my shoulder. 'Look . . . ' The even grey of the mist was darkening on one side . . . then the other. I'd known that in the end we'd catch sight of one bank—not both together. It was as if the lake was narrowing around us. Then I realized. Yes, the punt was moving, smoothly. There were no ripples, of course, because the water was moving with us . . . down towards the outflow, down towards the steady rushing sound: the culvert, and the grille.

I don't know what crowded through my brain then—thoughts of jumping out, maybe, holding Swan's head above water, splashing for the shore. If that's what I thought, it vanished the next moment. The banks were clear now; I could see the culvert, and there on one shore, already wading out into the shallows, was Antonin. He had a boat hook in his hand.

I picked up the punt pole, holding it near the centre, for balance. I felt like a knight who's not on horseback, trying to use his six-foot lance. I could see Antonin's face quite clearly, with its slowly spreading smile. He was waist deep now, and standing steady in the current, and his eyes were fixed on me. Where we were heading was going to take us just a boat hook's swing away. He was ready and waiting. I braced myself, and gave myself a little more length to jab with.

Then I thrust. The pole was so cumbersome he could see my move before it happened, but being waist deep slowed him down. He slapped the end of the pole aside

207

with the boat hook, but he lost his footing. With his other hand he grabbed my pole. For a mad long moment we were in a tug of war. I pulled back, jerked it, trying to dislodge him. But he had both hands on it now—he'd lost the boat hook—and he was hauling himself towards us, hand over hand. For a moment I didn't think, but tugged, and he came closer. Then I pushed the pole away with all my force.

He was expecting that, too. The pole went down and wedged a moment in the shallows, just enough for him to gain an arm's length on it. Then it was gone, and he was thrashing at us. With a dreamlike helplessness I saw one hand, then both of them, lock on the end of the punt.

The weight of him rocked us one way, and I staggered, on my hands and knees. It was only Swan who kept us from tipping over, hauling herself to the other end, keeping her weight low. The punt lurched, and started slewing round, circling end on end. Antonin had one arm up now; his face appeared above the end. That's when I flailed out, bringing a leg round to kick at his fingers again and again. First time I missed, then I connected. I stamped at his knuckles—white at first, then bleeding— but he didn't even flinch. He held on. Somewhere in his lifelong training, he'd dispensed with pain.

He'd got both arms up, as the punt spun round once more and steadied. It was moving fast, and all at once the sound of rushing water doubled, and redoubled, as the concrete walls closed in on either side. The punt seemed to kick forward, but still Antonin was gaining. The sudden lurch of speed seemed to help him, pushing the front down and forcing him up, because now one hand had grappled on a handhold. Half his body was in, and he was hauling, hauling. I lashed out, but weakly, as he raised his face, with that dead fixed grin on it, coming closer, inch by inch.

Swan shrieked. Antonin lurched forwards, and he had her by the leg. She was lying flat, but kicking and thrashing; Antonin held on. I kicked at him but he didn't even look. I was nothing to him, once he had his hands on Swan. She screamed and lashed out with the other foot, but he grabbed that, too, as the water foamed and the rush of it took us at bobsleigh speed. I had a glimpse of darkness coming at us, and both Antonin's hands like claws on Swan's leg, and I grabbed her as she slipped towards him.

Then the crash.

The punt reared up. White foam and darkness. For a second there was Antonin, and I thought he was standing upright—not quite walking, rather, *kneeling* on the water, because he hung there where the crash had thrown him and didn't fall back. As the punt slapped back down, the rusty grille buckled and began to give way, and we creaked through. I nearly toppled, but Swan grabbed me and with a startling strength held on, held on.

And Antonin? He was hanging there, and in the last moments we saw him he seemed to turn to watch us, still weirdly upright, still grinning. The current pulled him, and he turned as if to follow, but with a spike of the grille straight through his midriff all those hollow eyes could do was watch us slip away.

Then there was darkness, and roaring. As the tunnel swallowed us I lay flat, and pressed myself against Swan. We went into another small *forever* that was rushing and the smell of mud and water, moss and stone.

24

I t spat us out. One moment everything was darkness,
rushing past us, and all we could do was lie flat and
hold on. The next, there was light, and something
grating hard against the bottom of the punt, and we were
lurching, shuddering to a stop. The front had wedged on a
gravelly bank; the back swung halfway round till the force
of the stream got under it and levered it over, tipping Swan
and me out. We floundered, slipping, jamming our feet
among the slimy stones. I clutched a mossy boulder like a
long-lost friend.

We lay there, huddled in a cleft. The mist was getting
thick with drizzle, and the light was going. We were free.
Above us, up the bank, there was the regular whump and
hiss of cars passing. It was the ordinary world, and I'd
never been so glad to hear it. I don't know how long we
lay there in each other's arms. We could have lain there
forever, maybe. But no . . . We were both shivering. Swan
was still in the tatters of her ballet costume and she needed
dry clothes, soon.

Swan was on her feet before me, though her legs kept
buckling. Then I'd get under her and brace us, clutching a
branch or a bush, pant for a moment, then feel for a
foothold on the muddy slope. Or I'd slip and she'd grab
for me and stop me sliding. So we crawled our way up
through the weeds and brambles, and collapsed, just under
cover, on a grassy verge.

Whumph, hiss . . . There was one car a minute, maybe,
but they were moving fast. There'd be a halo of headlights

in the drizzle, and we'd shrink back, then the splash of
wheels on wet road, and the car was gone.

'Stay there,' I whispered.

'I'm coming,' she said as I scrambled to my feet. Then
we were waving at the dazzle . . . which zapped by. And
another, and another. I stepped out in the road, flagging,
flagging, and the next lights swerved a little to avoid me.
Just as I turned to swear at them, I saw the tail lights
slowing, then the reversing lights. A van, a white one. I
ran round to the driver's door and the window wound
down, and I looked up into a man's blunt face, and for a
moment there seemed to be no air to breathe any more.

It was one of Dom's men, the younger one. There
were thoughts in my head—should I run? should I
fight?—but my body was frozen. The other door
slammed.

'Amadeus! Get in, for God's sake.'

'Hob!'

'Don't worry,' he said. 'We're getting out of here.'

'We . . . ? What . . . ?'

'I'll explain,' said Hob. I hesitated. 'Trust me,' he said.

The other man leaned out. 'Come on, kid, move it!' It
was the look in his eyes clinched it: the man was
frightened too.

'Swan . . . ' I said. 'Help me.' And they did.

' . . . and Antonin's dead,' said Hob, as the van built up
speed. We were heading away from it all, no doubt about
it. 'In the sluice . . . '

'I know. We were there.'

He stared at me. 'Just don't ask,' I said.

Hob had climbed in the back with us, and was fishing
a towel from a bulging sports bag. 'You've packed!' said
Swan.

211

'I've been planning. Ever since Matty. And Antonin was on the edge, I could see it. I knew things were going to blow. Mind you,' he grinned, 'I'd reckoned without you two. And then the whole place went ape . . . ' He dug out a sweater and jeans and tossed them to Swan. My eyes had strayed to the back of the man's head Hob noticed. 'So I strolled over to our friend Dave here and said, *"Are you thinking what I'm thinking?"* '

Dave. How could Jarvis's partner be *Dave* . . . just like an ordinary bloke? 'Really? Easy as that?' I said.

'I watch people, see,' said Hob. 'That Jarvis, he was scary. Never smiled at us. He was Dom's man, OK—Dom just had to think the thought and Jarvis did it. Been with him for years, so I guess he'd got the habit. But I'd noticed Dave. Dave looked pretty uneasy, the way things were going. Isn't that right?'

Dave spoke over his shoulder. 'Too right. I mean,' he said, 'a job's a job, and I've done some dodgy numbers in my time, but . . . Jesus wept! That Dom—looks like a bloody bank clerk, but he'd sell his mother and not blink. Remember, I was his driver—went all over with him. I saw the kind of people he did business with. Russian Mafia, the lot. Scared me, I can tell you. Still, it's a living.' He stared at the white lines ahead for a moment. 'It was the night the Pan bloke snuffed it, that's what did for me. The way they dug a hole and dropped him in. And then that creepy funeral. I thought: that's it. Business is one thing, but this stuff's getting mental. Next chance I get, I'm out of here.'

Someone had panicked, so it seemed. It was when they found Jarvis with his skull staved in and Laura-Lee, bleeding buckets, and no sign of Dom. They phoned the ambulance, and the ambulance called the police. Of course, by the time someone spotted Dom up on the roof it was too late to stop them. There were going to be questions, big big questions. There was something about Dave that told me he didn't want to be around when that began.

'What about the others?' I said. 'Why only you two?'

'A few of them made a break for it,' Hob said. 'Most of them, they'll stay. That's the really sick thing. I heard them swearing *not to betray the memory of Antonin*. How gross is that! They'll clam up . . . ' Hob paused, his head on one side. 'Which is probably just as well, for you.'

The van's heater was working full blast now, and Swan had stopped shivering. 'You all right?' said Hob. 'Anything else we can do for you?'

Swan grinned. 'Hot soup? Fish and chips? I'm starving.'

'Let's get one thing clear,' Dave said. 'I'm not bleeding Father Christmas. I don't need you around, and I don't need you talking to anybody, either. You lot feel like talking to the police? Well, then. This van's gonna disappear, and so am I. This lift never happened, OK?'

'OK,' we said together.

'OK. So I came by a little windfall. Contents of the petty cash box. I don't suppose your old friend Dominic'll miss it. The next town, you get off. I'll give you just enough to find somewhere for the night, something to eat. Then you *vanish*. OK?'

'OK,' we said again.

'OK.'

It was dark at the windows now, and the sound of the engine was a steady drone. With the heat of the van, I was suddenly yawning. I put an arm around Swan. I felt her hesitate a moment, still stiff, then she let herself relax. *Mmmm*, she said. I heard her breathing settle as she fell asleep.

Funny how sometimes everything just comes together.

213

Neat. Almost too neat. I mean, that action sequence near the end, when I turn from the quiet observer to the vigilante hero? Like something from a Bond movie, that escape. Like wish fulfilment—the kind of thing your mind dreams up when something too dreadful has happened, there's no going back, when your brain can't imagine a way out, and if you faced the truth you might be screaming.

But I'm calm. Calm. I'm writing it down. Letter by letter, my finger rises, as if worked by clockwork. It hits a key; words appear on the screen. The whole story. And the audience gasps, to watch it unfolding in front of their eyes.

Full stop. Now there are cheers. And now my owner enters. Dom bows, to a ripple of appreciation from the audience, who are Laura-Lee, and Maisie, and Antonin too, and all the students. He turns to Albie too, who bows, as the attendants trundle out the box to pack up this latest working statue, this automaton—or is it? How do they work that single finger that can type a story, that makes some kind of sense? Do they notice that the finger is flexing now, waggling, trying to signal *No, no, no* . . .

And I wake, with a jolt of the van. No panic. Outside, there is the steady flow of a motorway barrier, the flicker of headlights . . . Once, the blue flash of a police car, heading the opposite way. There's a weight on my shoulder, and warmth: it's Swan, asleep, unguarded, leaning my way. I put an arm around her and she feels it, though she doesn't wake. I like the way she shifts and nestles closer. That's the amazing thing: her trusting me, still deep asleep.

No, this isn't stone time, not that weird forever present. Swan and me, we've got a future. I've got other plans

214

too. I want to see the Stone Saints. They'll look like amateurs now, but there's one thing they did that I'll never forget. It was that moment after the act, when one of them opened his eyes and let the other one touch. I could do that with Swan now. I know what it means. I'd like to find the Tin Man, and tell him that it's not impossible to find a heart. No, he'd just laugh at that. I'd like to say that he was lucky not to get his big break: at least he didn't end up like Matty the Pan. I'll send Mum a card, though not from Barcelona or Mauritius. And I'm going to track down Dad, too. I don't mean I'm looking for a happy-ever-after ending. He might be in hospital, or in some bedsit; knowing what's happened to me won't make him any less depressed. Or maybe it will. Whatever he's been through, it won't have been as crazy as the places I've been.

And I'll have Swan with me. She's been right down there, in the bad place. He'll see that. She'll understand him, too. I want him to know that I'm proud of her, and that she's proud of me.

I'm not imagining all this, am I? It's not just another of my dreams? Will I ever be quite sure again?

Maybe not. But it'll have to do.